PREACHING TO THE CORPSE

Preaching to the Corpse

Roberta Isleib

WHEELER
CHIVERS

This Large Print edition is published by Wheeler Publishing, Waterville, Maine, USA and by BBC Audiobooks Ltd, Bath, England.
Wheeler Publishing, a part of Gale, Cengage Learning.

The text of this Large Print edition is unabridged.
Other aspects of the book may vary from the original edition.
Set in 16 pt. Plantin.
Printed on permanent paper.

LIBRARY OF CONGRESS CATALOGING-IN-PUBLICATION DATA

Isleib, Roberta.
   Preaching to the corpse / by Roberta Isleib.
     p. cm.
   "An advice column mystery" — T.p. verso.
   ISBN-13: 978-1-59722-750-6 (pbk. : alk. paper)
   ISBN-10: 1-59722-750-1 (pbk. : alk. paper)
     1. Clinical psychologists — Fiction. 2. Advice columnists — Fiction. 3. New England — Fiction. 4. Clergy — Fiction. 5. Large type books. I. Title.
   PS3609.S57P74 2008
   813'.6—dc22   2008002756

BRITISH LIBRARY CATALOGUING-IN-PUBLICATION DATA AVAILABLE
Published in 2008 in the U.S. by arrangement with The Berkley Publishing Group, a member of Penguin Group (USA) Inc.
Published in 2008 in the U.K. by arrangement with The Berkley Publishing Group, a member of Penguin Group (USA) Inc.
U.K. Hardcover: 978 1 405 64592 8 (Chivers Large Print)
U.K. Softcover: 978 1 405 64593 5 (Camden Large Print)

Printed in the United States of America
1 2 3 4 5 6 7 12 11 10 09 08

For my friends at the
First Congregational Church,
Madison, Connecticut,

and

for the Reverend Andy Schramm

ACKNOWLEDGMENTS

Many thanks to: Mary Jane Isleib, Phyllis Kaletsky, Jack and Jane Novick for thoughts on condo life; Chris Falcone, Angelo Pompano, Cindy Warm, and Chris Woodside for their steady support and insight; Susan Hubbard for her humor, perspective, and friendship; Susan Cerulean and Jeff Chanton for encouragement and comments on early drafts; the Reverend Gina Finocchiaro for the minister's discretionary fund; the generous and sometimes scary Poison Lacy, Luci Zahray, for the lily of the valley; Dr. Doug Lyle for medical information, cheerfully rendered; Dr. Joel Allison for thoughts on divinity school candidates; Marcia Stone for the history of the church; the honorable Judge Pat Clifford and Officer Timothy Bernier from the Guilford Police Department — as always, mistakes in police procedure are purely mine!

And thank you to independent editor

Nora Cavin, above all for her insistence that I let the characters lead the way; the great team at Berkley Prime Crime, particularly my thoughtful, supportive editor Katie Day, and fireball publicist Catherine Milne; and my agent, the fabulous Paige Wheeler, her smart associate Laney Becker, and all the other good people at Folio Literary Agency.

I couldn't carry on with any of this without the generous, hard-working, fun-loving mystery community — especially my New England buddies and my Sisters in Crime. And thanks to my dear friends in Connecticut, including the staff and members at the First Congregational Church — of course any resemblance to the Shoreline Congregational Church is purely fictional. Happy three-hundredth birthday!

As ever, I'm grateful to my family, especially John: supporter, critic, treasured friend, and partner.

Roberta Isleib
May 2007

- *In 1650 the Hammonassett territory was added, having been given to Mr. Whitfield by Mr. Fenwick, the Indians from whom he purchased it promising to leave the locality, but reserving the right to hunt and fish there. All the settlement east of East River became known as East Guilford. In the Guilford settlement the first church was gathered June 19, 1643.*
- *After the death of the Reverend John Hart, the society, at a meeting held in April 1731, voted: "To call five ministers to carry on the day of fasting and prayer, and to advise us respecting calling a man in the work of the ministry in this place." The Reverend Abraham Todd was invited to settle, but as the vote of the society was not quite unanimous, he declined.*
- *The sexton tolled the church bell when anyone died, and after a pause, struck on the bell the age of the person, in groups of ten strikes*

> *"till the age was counted,"* then after a pause, struck once more if for a man and twice if a woman.

From
HISTORY OF THE FIRST
CONGREGATIONAL CHURCH,
1707–1955,
compiled by Mary Scranton Evarts

CHAPTER 1

The phone jarred me out of a restless sleep.

"Dr. Butterman?"

I groped for the clock radio. 12:18. It was pitch dark and my mind swirled with dream riffs.

"Rebecca? Are you there? It's Reverend Wesley Sandifer. Sorry to wake you." His voice sounded tremulous and strained.

My lizard brain — home of primitive fears and fight-or-flight reactions — kicked in: "Minister plus phone call after midnight equals disaster." Years of training as a clinical psychologist couldn't protect me from a rush of nightmarish possibilities and dread.

My sister, Janice? My niece, Brittany? My dearest girlfriends, Angie or Annabelle? The image of a terrible car wreck, pulsing red flesh and twisted metal, flashed into mind. But why would any of the people I loved most be driving in the middle of the night? And how the hell would Reverend Wesley know? My heart pounded and my hands slicked up so much I almost dropped the phone.

"What's wrong?" I whispered fiercely. "What happened?"

"I'm sorry to bother you at this hour," he said again, his voice growing shrill. "It's not what you're thinking. I need your help."

I logged a reassuring observation: Besides the comforting words, he hadn't cloaked himself in the sorry-to-have-to-tell-you-this tone that preceded breaking bad news.

"We have a situation." He cleared his throat and paused.

"Could you be a little more specific?" I asked, feeling the adrenaline sluicing through my veins shift to annoyance at being woken up and frightened out of my gourd.

"I'm going to put Detective Meigs on, if that's okay." I heard rustling and mumbling then Meigs's voice.

"Dr. Butterman? I'm with the Reverend Wesley Sandifer at the emergency medical clinic on exit 59."

I hadn't expected to hear Detective Meigs's deep rumble anytime soon — not ever, really. Midnight observation number two: He and I were back to formal salutations.

We'd made an unexpected connection after I stumbled into one of his cases last fall. But I'm single and he isn't. End of drama, curtain falls, as my practical friend Annabelle would say. Only it wasn't really the end, if you counted flashbacks and dreams in which the sighing damsel (me) was rescued over and over by the muscular though well-padded redheaded cop (him). It was enough to make any card-carrying feminist cringe.

The partial fog in my mind began to lift. "Is Reverend Wesley hurt?"

"Not exactly," said Meigs, sighing heavily. "You're a member of the Shoreline Congregational Church?"

He was looking for religion at midnight? I was too tired to answer anything but "yes."

"There's been a suspicious death," Meigs said. "We'd like to get this sorted out before the news hits the coffee shops in the morning. Can you possibly come down? The reverend insists he won't talk to anyone but you," he continued, his exasperation plain. Clearly he thought all of this was utter crapola. I had to agree. I'm a psychologist, not a detective. Or a lawyer — if that's what Wesley needed.

My brain shifted one gear higher, trying to put the pieces together. "Good God! Was

Wesley involved in the death?"

"He called it in," said Meigs, not saying what everyone knows from TV crime shows: Whoever finds the body is a damn good suspect.

"Trust me, Reverend Wesley wouldn't kill anyone." Another shock wave of fear rocketed through me. "Who died?"

"Lacy Bailes."

I felt the air whoosh out of my lungs, as if I'd been socked in the gut. It couldn't be. Maybe he had it wrong; maybe it was a stranger. I was just getting to know Lacy — a big woman with a forbidding exterior, but all heart underneath. My mouth watered with budding nausea.

"When can you get here?" Meigs asked. "Should I send a patrol car?"

I didn't want to get involved with another tragedy; I'd barely recovered from the stress of my next-door neighbor's death in September. "What am I supposed to do once I'm there?"

Meigs was silent for a moment. "Reverend Wesley says he'll talk to me if you're here. Look, he hasn't been arrested. Yet. You might make a big difference with that."

"I'll be down in half an hour."

I pulled on my warmest sweats, heavy gray fleece pants and a hoodie whose princess seams could not disguise the seven pounds of winter padding I'd packed on earlier in the season. Being held at gunpoint by a lunatic back in September had had the effect of increasing my appetite and decreasing my self-control.

I glanced in the mirror, then stripped the sweats back off, exchanging the Michelin Man look for jeans and a holiday sweater, refusing to think about why I would spend more than one minute dressing for our minister and the local ER. Refusing to think about what could have happened to Lacy Bailes. Grabbing my purse and a small notebook, I headed out to the garage.

A plume of exhaust drifted under the Honda as I backed into the street. Babette Finster's white Christmas lights glowed softly on the large holly bushes on either side of her front walk. I could feel the hairs in my nose freeze up before the heater kicked in. It was unusually cold for December and clear enough to see a picture-book display of stars. We'd had six inches of snow in the last week and not one flake had melted.

I turned the radio up, looking for company. An all-night station was playing a run of sappy Christmas tunes. I suffered through "I Saw Mommy Kissing Santa Claus," then

Paul McCartney crooning about having a wonderful Christmastime. He was a Beatle for God's sake, an icon of rock 'n' roll. Couldn't his manager — or his wife — have saved him before he sank to the lowest common denominator of holiday schlock?

McCartney's faux cheeriness couldn't push back the worried possibilities that waited to surge forward if I gave them any room. Reverend Wesley a murderer? It didn't seem possible that he would hurt anyone, certainly not Lacy. They were always cordial in my presence. In fact he'd handpicked her to head the search committee currently working to find a new assistant minister. This was one of Wesley's strong points — persuading laypeople to take up the heavy yoke of church business in return for no pay and lots of second-guessing from the rest of the congregation.

I felt a little twinge of small-minded dismay. What did he want from me? *Enough!* I ordered. *You'll find out when you get there.* My mind glided seamlessly to Detective Meigs. What was the status of his wife's illness? *STOP! STOP!*

I turned off Route 1, drove under I-95, and pulled into the Shoreline Emergency Clinic's driveway. Quite a few cars were parked in the front visitors' lot, even though most people in our little Connecticut town are fast asleep at this hour.

I picked my way across the blacktop, boots crunching on small pyramids of compacted snow — and slipped on a patch of ice. Arms flailing, I crashed onto my butt. A sharp pain radiated from my buttock and down my right thigh. I lay on the pavement, moaning, and assessed the damage: bruised hip and pride. I rolled to my knees and staggered up.

Meigs was waiting at the front door, the smile on his lips not quite reaching his worried eyes.

"You all right?"

Was he interested in the sequelae of my awkward landing or the deeper psychological ramifications of this past fall's events? I chose to grunt out "fine." Meigs looked more tired than when I'd seen him several months ago: cheeks a little more chiseled, circles under his eyes a darker hue. His close-cropped curls glinted gold-red with a spritz of silver under the bright lights of the front portico.

Leave it, Rebecca, I scolded myself. Like a dog that had gotten ahold of someone else's bone. "What happened?" I asked curtly. "Why am I really here?"

"Your reverend seems to be flipping out,"

Meigs said. He strode ahead of me through the waiting area, detouring around a woman vomiting into a trashcan and an older man with his head wrapped in a bloody towel. We pushed through a set of wooden doors marked *staff only* and walked down the hallway toward the back of the clinic. "He called 911 and reported an emergency. He says he stopped into Lacy Bailes's condominium and found her very sick. The EMTs brought them both here."

"So she isn't dead!" I exclaimed, weak with relief.

"She's definitely dead. They worked on her for almost two hours before they gave up. We haven't been able to get a sensible word out of Reverend Wesley since, and he insisted on speaking to you. The doc on call has been too busy to formally evaluate him." He glanced back at me and grimaced. "We had three choices: Put him in jail, take him to the Yale emergency room, or give him a half a Valium and call you." He shrugged. "We're trying you first."

I stopped still. "But if Lacy was ill, why would you even consider putting Wesley in jail?"

Meigs turned to face me, lowering his voice. "She had all the classic symptoms of a heart attack. But the doc got suspicious

18

about poison and called me in. We can't be certain until the autopsy results come back. That could be days — we need permission from next of kin, and nothing happens on a damn weekend. Obviously, I'm exaggerating about an arrest tonight, but it's imperative that your reverend tell us everything he knows."

We rounded the corner and passed through another set of double doors, these painted deep blue. Reverend Wesley was slumped in a blue upholstered chair in a mini waiting area, his white shirt rumpled and marked with rings of sweat. His eyes were closed and he held a dog-eared copy of *People* magazine on his lap.

"Wesley?"

As the minister popped up to hold out his hand, the magazine dropped to the floor, open to an article about celebrity cheating. "The Ultimate Betrayal!" the headline brayed.

"Thank goodness you're here."

I squeezed his fingers gently. "What happened? Are you all right?" With most people in this situation, I would have rushed forward to offer a hug. Reverend Wesley's body language didn't welcome that kind of consolation.

"Let's find a room where we can talk more

comfortably," said Meigs. He strode down the hall, poked his head into one of the doors, then waved us down. "Can I get you some coffee? Water?"

I almost smiled. Flight attendant Meigs: Who'd have guessed? Wesley and I shook our heads as we settled into more plastic chairs on either side of an examining table. Wesley's gaze shifted to the metal stirrups and quickly back to the floor. Meigs perched on a rolling stool near the medicine cabinet. I reached diagonally across the white-paper-covered table to shorten the distance between Wesley's hand and mine.

Meigs pulled out his Palm Pilot and cleared his throat. "Start from the beginning please, Reverend, and take us through what happened tonight."

Wesley patted his lips and combed through his hair with his fingers. His nails, ordinarily as fastidious as a hand model's, were filthy.

"I had an appointment to talk with Lacy at eight." His eyes filled and he snuffled into the back of his hand. I rummaged through my purse, extracted a tissue, and handed it over.

"You had an appointment to talk about what?" Meigs prompted.

"The search committee, of course," said Reverend Wesley. He closed his eyes, clenched his hands on the examining table, and lowered his forehead to his fists.

"Lacy was chairing the committee charged with locating an assistant pastor to serve under Reverend Wesley," I said to Meigs. "Our former assistant found a new job and left rather precipitously. But nothing moves quickly in a church bureaucracy. And we have a large congregation. It's been quite a stretch, hasn't it, trying to meet everyone's needs?" I patted the white paper on the table. "We do have an intern," I added inanely.

Wesley lifted his head and stared at me, his pupils dilated. *Valium or shock?* I wondered.

"Will you take over as chair?"

I sucked in a deep breath, noticing the sharp tang of his body odor and a waft of disinfectant. "Wesley, listen to me. The search committee is the least of your problems." I glanced quickly at Meigs. Leaning closer, I squeezed the minister's wrist and whispered: "You could be arrested for murder here."

"No!" he said, shaking me off, a glazed look in his eyes. "Of course I didn't kill her! She was barely conscious when I got there. She was having trouble breathing. That's why I called the clinic."

21

"How did you get into the house, Reverend?" Meigs asked. "It doesn't sound like she was in any condition to answer her door."

Wesley's cheeks flushed pink. "She was expecting me. When she didn't respond to my knocking, I went in. I had a feeling something was wrong."

"So you arrived at eight, discovered her on the couch a few minutes later, and called 911 right after that?"

Wesley nodded, the movements of his head a little sloppy. "We were so close to filling the position. We have two interviews scheduled: Paul Cashman on Monday; he's our intern who's finishing up at Yale this spring." He glanced at his watch and pressed his palm to his eyes. "And Ellen Dark's on her way down from New Hampshire, if she isn't already here. She's spending the weekend in Madison. She wants to check out the area. The committee is going to interview her Sunday night." He spread his delicate but grubby hands wide, a beseeching look on his face. "Both highly qualified, of course. If we put this off any longer, we'll lose them and have to start from scratch. We simply can't go on without another minister."

Meigs was right — Wesley did appear to

22

be losing his mind. "We could always hire someone temporarily —"

"No!" he yelped. "Don't you understand? We've already done the work!"

I patted his arm, cooing softly until he settled down.

"I found her," he whimpered. "When I got to her house, she was almost — dead." His hand wandered to his chest, plucking at his wool scarf. His eyes welled with tears. "Will you do it? Join the committee, I mean?" He began to cough, a sharp bark, thick with phlegm. Meigs handed him a small box of tissues from the counter and rolled his stool back a few inches.

"When you arrived, she looked sick?"

"I already told you," Wesley snapped. He took a ragged breath. "I'm sorry. She was so pale. And her breathing was labored and her skin was clammy." His eyes bulged as he coughed again. "It looked like a heart attack."

"Did you try CPR?" I asked.

He stared blankly. "I learned CPR twenty-five years ago — never took a refresher. I was afraid to hurt her. Besides, nothing I could do was going to bring her back. Nothing." With his hands to his mouth, the last words were mumbled. "So I called 911." His head wobbled, as if the weight was too much for his neck.

"Did you see anyone on the way in or out of her apartment?" Meigs asked.

Wesley shrugged his shoulders. "No. Will you" — he looked at me and hacked helplessly — "join the committee?"

"Of course I'll help."

Meigs frowned and tipped his head toward the hall. I excused myself and followed him out.

"I think he's suffering from a version of post-traumatic shock," I said to Meigs, who was leaning against the wall. "He's not thinking straight."

He raised his eyebrows, one a quarter inch higher than the other.

"He wants to appoint me to the vacant slot on the search committee. Why would he be so worried about that at a time like this?"

Meigs straightened, spreading his hands. "Spell it out."

"Lacy Bailes chaired the group that was choosing a new assistant minister." I bit my lip, organizing my thoughts; he'd want to know everything. "Because we had an intern coming on board from the Yale Divinity School, we skipped the interim minister step this time."

He scratched his head and shrugged. "I'm

Catholic," he said. "By upbringing anyway. We don't choose our priests; they're sent from on high. You'll have to explain the procedure."

I sighed. "When a minister leaves, the church is supposed to choose an interim pastor. This guy — or woman — helps the congregation mourn the old minister and make an emotional attachment to the new leader."

Meigs shook his head. "Greek to me."

"Put it this way, the interim pastor is sort of like a foster parent. Churches that don't follow the protocol run the risk of ending up with an attachment disorder." I was beginning to sound like a pamphlet from the church's central office.

"So let me get this straight," Meigs said, yawning and pulling on his left ear, "you were supposed to hire someone to help you recover from your previous minister?"

"Not only this particular minister," I said impatiently. Right now it seemed like a stupid process and impossible to explain. "It's a specialty — clergy who go from church to church for short periods of transition. We call them interim pastors."

"Sounds to me like it's the interim ministers who have attachment disorders," said Meigs.

I stared at him, then glanced at my watch. "One-thirty in the morning and you're a comedian. I'd like to know why my pastor went to this woman's home for a meeting on a Friday night."

"We'd both like to know that," Meigs said briskly. "And then an hour later she turns up dead. What can you tell me about Ms. Bailes?"

I sucked in a breath. Funny how you can see someone every Sunday, even talk with them in coffee hour, and still hardly know them at all. But I liked her. My eyes teared up. And I'd given Wesley my only Kleenex.

"She was single. She works — worked — for an insurance company in Hartford." What if I'd known her better, taken more time? *STOP!* I wasn't going down that road with Lacy: It'd brought nothing but agony with my dead neighbor. A tear started down my cheek. "I'm so tired. I can't really think."

Meigs frowned. "Fine, we'll talk in the morning. Meanwhile, do you think the Reverend's gone bonkers?"

I blotted my face with my sleeve and cracked a small smile. "You won't find that diagnosis in the DSM-V. But probably not a bad idea to keep him for observation overnight and get an official psychiatric consult."

"And not a terrible idea to have you sit on that committee," said Meigs. "Just don't start thinking you're on the case. Or the clock." He pressed on before I could cut him off. "You're a damn good observer and your minister seems to trust you. And I have a feeling there are going to be gnarly confidentiality issues before we're through. Think it over. I'll check in with you tomorrow."

He wheeled back into the exam room. I was dismissed. "Can I say good night to the reverend?" The door clicked shut behind him.

"What do you think happened to Lacy?" I called. My voice echoed in the empty corridor.

Outside, the wind had picked up from merely sharp to biting. I minced back over the icy blacktop to my car, feeling a dull ache in my hip. I drove home slowly, passing the church on the way. Spotlights illuminated green wreaths with red bows on massive wooden doors, and candles gleamed through the wavy window glass, projecting an aura of peace and beauty.

Wouldn't *that* be shot to hell by morning?

CHAPTER 2

Wearing flannel pajamas, L.L.Bean gumboots, and my ex-husband Mark's faded blue terrycloth robe, I limped out the front door to snatch the *New York Times* from its curbside box. My friend Angie recently threatened to commandeer the robe and replace it at Christmas with something from Victoria's Secret.

"Wearing your ex's bathrobe is bad romantic karma," Angie said.

"Wearing something sexy that no one but me sees is far worse," I replied.

On the way back up the steps, I noticed a flyer wedged under the storm door. I unfolded it and began to read.

Dear residents:
Yesterday I received a letter signed "Irate resident of Soundside Home-owners Association." The writer complained about the strings of

28

lights on the pine trees and bushes in front of several residents' homes and accused the Board of governing by selective rules. They described us as "frauds who cater to our pals." Obviously this author hasn't read the bylaws that were approved, published, and distributed in November. Page 17, section b: Decorations are allowed on the lawns and shrubbery between Thanksgiving and New Year's, which is THE HOLIDAY SEASON. My official response to this person is next time have the courtesy to sign your complaint. My unofficial response? "Bah Humbug!"

Harrison Nelson, president, Soundside Homeowners Association

My most annoying neighbor, Mrs. Dunbarton, has been on the warpath since losing her bid for election as condo association president last month. The unsigned missive had to be her work. I had the urge to run to Wal-Mart and purchase ropes of huge colored bulbs to string across my bushes. The retro look was back in style anyway, but Mrs. Dunbarton preferred white lights only, and preferably indoors. *That would drive her mad,* I thought, smiling.

29

I started a pot of coffee and popped a sesame bagel into the toaster oven. My hip ached and a nasty black bruise was taking shape where I'd had the altercation with the blacktop. My brain felt fuzzy from a short night riddled by disruptive dreams about our minister and poor dead Lacy. Not to mention Meigs. That dream sharpened into better focus: I'd been a maiden trapped in a castle turret and he was a horseman in a coat of mail. Arggghh . . .

I left messages at the church for Reverend Wesley and at the police department for Detective Meigs, then pulled a bag of apples out of the fridge. The annual Christmas potluck and carol sing was scheduled for this evening, and I'd signed up to bring a pie. I peeled eight apples, managing to skin the last in one long link. When I was a kid, our next-door neighbor told me I could discover my future married name by tossing an intact peel over my shoulder. I picked up the skin and threw it, just as Spencer rounded the corner into the kitchen. He yelped and arched away from the broken peel, radiating reproach as only a cat can.

"Sorry, buddy," I called after his retreating form. The biggest piece of skin looked something like an *L,* which meant nothing to me. Yet. I scooped it into the trash. "Who needs a second husband anyway?" I called after Spencer.

It had taken months and many therapy sessions to get over the first one. Angie has always maintained that the only real reason for a husband is to set up the Christmas tree. And now that the new self-installing stands are available, even the biggest tree practically mounts itself. I snickered: No pun intended.

I sprinkled the apples with sugar and cinnamon, squeezed lemon juice into the bowl, and stirred. Then I measured out two cups of flour and mixed in milk and canola oil, feeling sad about Lacy. What information would Meigs want? I'd felt an instant bond with her after our first conversation about my advice column. When folks find out I'm *Bloom!* magazine's answer to Ann Landers as well as being a therapist, they often produce a problem — thinly disguised as that of a neighbor or friend. Not so Lacy.

"It's draining to be the one with the answers," she'd said, "but also a beautiful calling."

"I do love solving problems in two paragraphs or less," I admitted. "Of course psychotherapy is the best way for people to make serious changes, but it's awful hard work. For both me and the patient. With an advice column, there's absolutely no back talk!" We both laughed.

Then Lacy explained that she was a recovering alcoholic — fourteen years sober — with a mission to support and advise any other poor souls pulling themselves out of the same deep hole. "Actually, some people might say I'm better at badgering than supporting." Another round of laughter.

The whine of a snowblower outside my window jolted me back to the present. Our condo handyman, Bernd Becker, was clearing the sidewalks leading to the clubhouse. I puzzled over Meigs's comment last night that the attending doctor suspected poison. Why the hell would someone poison Lacy? Maybe it was a heart attack after all. Maybe in the stress and chaos of the season, Meigs and the ER doc had jumped the gun.

I rolled the piecrust between two pieces of waxed paper, then peeled off the top layer and patted the dough into a glass pan, thinking about Wesley's request. I believed I could be useful to the search committee. They would be stunned by Lacy's death. They might be able to use a professional to sort through feelings of grief and shock and then move on with their job. And maybe I could slow down Reverend Wesley's panicked plan for hiring the new minister. No reason we shouldn't get him some temporary help. Hopefully, last night's adamant objection had been fueled by shock and Valium.

Meanwhile, I would be happy to feed observations to Jack Meigs. Blushing, I dumped the apples into the pan, rolled out the top crust, plopped it on top of the pie, and crimped it closed. Why had Meigs agreed to Wesley's request to call me in the middle of the night? After slashing vents in the crust, I slid the pie into the oven and dialed Annabelle Hart.

"Are we still on for lunch? I've got a situation I need to discuss."

"Definitely. Noon at the Hidden Kitchen."

I hung up, visions of a cheese omelet with home fries and maybe bacon on the side dancing in my head — *STOP!* A *salad.* Definitely.

I trust Annabelle for her sensible perspective on just about anything. She's a social worker with a reputation in the Yale psychiatry department as a bit of a flake. Which only means that her powerful intuition and preference for using sand trays and journaling in therapy don't fit comfortably into the medical model. She's done psychological evaluations for prospective ordination candidates from the Yale Divinity School for years. If anyone had insight into the private tickings of a minister, it would be her.

While I waited for the pie to bake, I fired up my laptop, determined to knock off an advice column before lunch. I moonlight as Dr. Aster, *Bloom!* online magazine's expert on heartbreak and love. Jillian, my young editor, had specifically requested that the columns this month reflect holiday themes. Finding appropriate problems wouldn't be hard: By the look of my E-mail box, not too many people manage to enjoy this season — there are more Grinches out there than elves. I sorted through the possibilities, quickly brainstorming answers, feeling like Clark Kent about to morph into Superman. Then I copied a reader's letter into my E-mail to Jillian and began to type the reply.

Dear Dr. Aster:
The holidays are here, and as usual, I'm ready to kill my stepmother. Since marrying my father ten years ago, she's run the show. Christmas is "her holiday" and she's completely unwilling to compromise. We're welcome to gather at her house with her family, but she won't consider coming to one of our homes. She certainly won't consider

34

spending time with my deceased mother's family — though they and my father were very close. She takes good care of my dad and he hasn't been well — but this is sticking in our collective craw. In fact, I can't stop thinking of her selfishness and it's ruining my Christmas season. Can you help — fast?

Sincerely,
Yelping at Yule in Yonkers

Dear Yelping:
Ah, the hellidays. Bing Crosby didn't do us any favors by suggesting that a white Christmas translates directly to harmony and joy. As with weddings, holiday stress can bring out the worst in people who normally love each other. Add to the mix folks who aren't related and aren't sure they care for each other one whit — emotional mayhem can ensue. You are justified in feeling that your stepmother's approach isn't fair — she isn't even pretending! If you have a good relationship — and it sounds like you might — invite her to a few sessions with a family counselor to clear the air. Or take her for

35

lunch or coffee in the New Year and ask to have a talk. Let her know how much you'd appreciate a compromise, one Christmas dinner out of three at your home, for example.

But wait! You asked for FAST help. Behavioral psychologists sometimes use this technique to reduce circular thinking. Put a rubber band around your wrist. When the intrusive thoughts about your stepmother pop up, snap the rubber band and tell yourself to STOP! Then repeat your last sentence as needed: She takes good care of my dad. She takes good care of my dad . . . Good luck and try to enjoy the celebration!

The timer went off and I pulled the pie from the oven, golden brown with steam drifting from the vents. I wondered if the minister would make it home from the hospital in time for the potluck. Why *was* he at Lacy's place on a Friday night? Could they have been involved? I pictured this briefly — the gangly, pale limbs of our minister entangled with Lacy Bailes's ample thighs. *STOP!* Too late. I imagined his lips, waxy with lip balm, snuggling the folds in his parishioner's neck. Even a series of vigorous rubber-band snaps wouldn't wipe this image away.

After showering and dressing quickly, I drove down Route 1 to the Hidden Kitchen, a cozy home-style restaurant tucked into the back of a small strip mall, directly adjacent to a gym with floor-to-ceiling windows. I almost never regret choosing comfort food over weightlifting. Annabelle was already seated at a table for two, with a view of the sweating exercisers just around the corner in one direction and the sweating chefs in the other.

I stopped to study the blackboard specials and then went to join Annabelle. "You look fantastic," I said, bending down to kiss her. "The haircut took off ten years." At Angie's urging, both Annabelle and I had succumbed to the scissors of a hair virtuoso in New Haven. He gleefully carved off her braid, leaving a flattering halo of curls. In my opinion, he'd been far less successful with mine — a choppy, gamine style that made me look like I was trying too hard to be hip.

"What are you having? My eye's on the peach melba Belgian waffle," she said as I took my seat.

"I should probably order a salad," I said, picking up the menu. "I'm going to the church supper tonight where I'm sure to overdo it."

"Seize the day," Annabelle said with a smile. "Personally, I'd hate to think my last meal was a plate of lettuce."

The waitress, a middle-aged woman in jeans and a navy HK polo, appeared at the table breathless and expectant. "What'll it be, ladies?"

I closed the menu and handed it over. "I'll have the stuffed pepper special, blue cheese on the salad."

Annabelle chuckled and ordered her waffle. "That's my girl. Now what's up? You've got me curious."

I whispered the short version of the Shoreline Congregational Church tragedy — in truth, the short version was all I knew.

"He came to visit and she died within the hour?"

"At the Shoreline clinic." I nodded. "Isn't that awful? The poor woman. They think she might have been poisoned. *Poisoned.* Reverend Wesley was so upset — he wouldn't talk with Meigs unless I came in."

"Why in the world would he ask for you?"

"He wants me to join the search committee. In fact he wants me to take over as chair."

Annabelle scratched her head and

frowned. "One of his parishioners has been murdered and he's worried about the search committee?"

"I guess he feels comfortable with me." I began to fold my napkin into a fan. "When Wesley's wife left, the deacons asked him to consult with me. He seemed to be in a bit of a downward spiral." I smiled ruefully and replaced the napkin on the table. "He was convinced he was doing just fine. And he seemed to feel awkward talking with one of his own flock. So I gave him a referral — to you actually. I'm assuming you haven't heard from him?"

"Not yet."

"Do you think I should tell the cops about that meeting?"

"Of course! Tell them you had one exploratory conversation with Wesley and referred him out. If he didn't tell you anything confidential, what would be the point of holding back?"

I nodded, shredding the edge of the napkin. "Meigs thinks it's a good idea that I join the search group — maybe I'll pick up something useful about Lacy's death from the inner circle." I laughed weakly; the plan sounded absurd spoken aloud. "I'm to keep him posted if I hear anything that might have a bearing on the case, but it's not a partnership. Obviously."

Her eyebrows knit into one worried line. "Are you listening to yourself, Rebecca? Why would the possibility of a partnership even occur to you?" She cleared her throat and reached for the tip of her phantom braid, seeming surprised that it wasn't there. "Are you still having nightmares?"

"Every once in a while. Not often."

Besides my therapist, Annabelle has heard more about my abduction last September than anyone else. She even persuaded me to act it out with figurines in one of her sand trays. And then wipe the whole thing clean with a miniature rake — a surprising satisfaction.

My gaze wandered to the oversized lighthouse painted on the wall. How to explain without protesting too much? "Reverend Wesley seems to think I'd be a calming influence on the committee. And Meigs thinks I might hear something that will help him with the case. But mostly, it's Lacy." My eyes teared up. "She was one of the good guys."

"Is Wesley a suspect?" she asked.

"Of course Meigs wouldn't say that directly. But he did ask if Wesley and Lacy had been involved."

"And —"

"I don't think so," I said. "Beverly — that's his wife — left him a couple of months ago. There's been the usual gossip about the reasons for the split, but he strikes me as a straight arrow. I'm going to the church supper tonight so I'll have the chance to ask around."

"You've been invited onto the search committee," Annabelle said sternly, "not recruited for the police department."

"I know, I know," I said, frowning. "But if I can help ease Wesley off the hook, it helps the whole church."

Annabelle's eyes narrowed but I was saved from further scrutiny by the arrival of lunch. I cut off a bite of pepper stuffed with sausage, onions, and rice, and spooned a dollop of tomato sauce on top.

"Mmm, so good. Thanks for talking me out of the rabbit food."

Annabelle grinned, dabbing a spot of whipped cream off her chin. "It wasn't exactly a tough sell."

When I'd finished most of the pepper and half the salad — I could eat salad any time — I laid my fork on the table. "I've always wondered why a person would choose to be a minister. Honestly, the idea of someone thinking God picked them out and called them bothers me. That voice could be anything: a figment of his imagination, nagging from his mother, plain old grandiosity, even psychosis. And does the call come by cell phone? A landline? Maybe E-mail?"

Annabelle sipped her coffee. "It's not so different from anyone else trying to find her life's work. Some psychologists enter the field because their own family is crazy, and sure, some ministers are missing a wing nut." She poured syrup on the remains of her waffle and pointed at me with her fork. "But you're wondering if your pastor is capable of murder."

My cell phone buzzed indicating a text message had been delivered, a very unusual event for me. I glanced at the screen.

Meet u at station in 20 . . . Meigs.

"He wants me to swing by the police station," I said.

"Who?"

I held up the phone and Annabelle leaned forward, squinting at the screen. "Meigs? He knows how to send a text message?"

"Apparently," I said, feeling a wave of heat spread across my face. Guilty as charged, I could imagine her thinking. Guilty of what? I plucked my bag from the back of the chair and reached for the check. Annabelle grabbed my hand in both of hers and ran one finger across the knuckles.

"How's his wife doing?" she asked gently.

"I haven't a clue. It was one in the morning and we weren't really catching up on social niceties." I sighed and slumped back in the chair. "Look, it's not a date. He just wants information. He doesn't know the church or the people."

"I don't want to see you get hurt."

I stood up and went around the table to hug her. "Me either."

CHAPTER 3

On the short hop to the police station, I thought more about poor Lacy. And poor distraught Wesley. It didn't seem fair to automatically connect the dots between those two. He was just the unlucky bastard who found her. But how had he managed to find her? Was she in the habit of leaving her door unlocked? Was he in the habit of walking right in? Had she died a painless death —

I forced my mind back to Reverend Wesley. Some clergy seem to actually feel the presence of God inside. They are happy — no, compelled — to share the Good News. Other ministerial types seem to wear their religious cloak as a thin veneer over their ordinary human darkness. Their godliness feels brittle, like a clear caramel coating I tasted on my honeymoon in Paris. The waiter tapped it with a spoon and the shell splintered into a dozen pieces, revealing the foie gras — fat liver — underneath.

Had something cracked our minister open like French caramel?

I parked in front of the red brick police station and sat a moment longer in the car, the engine ticking and my heart beating too fast. I had to cut back on caffeine.

Meigs met me in the waiting area and I tromped behind him to his office. The hallway carpet was stained with melting salt and ice. His cubicle was just as I remembered: a jumble of institutional furniture and messy piles of paper. It smelled of stale coffee and wet wool. The photograph of Meigs with his wife and dog still stood on the file cabinet, but buried deeper behind a stack of manila folders with colored tabs. At this point, a visitor could only see his wife from her substantial chest up and only the dog's eyes and ears. Not really fair for such a small woman to have big breasts. Not to mention those gorgeous brown eyes. *Not to mention Lou Gehrig's disease,* I scolded myself.

Meigs gestured to the chair just inside the door and perched on his desk, one leg swinging. A little closer than he needed to be.

"Thanks for coming," he said, with a slight frown. "I'd like to finish up with what

45

we didn't get to last night."

"You're welcome. Have you had word from Wesley? I left a message at the church but he hasn't called back."

Meigs shrugged. "They released him from the clinic this morning. I assume he went home."

"He's not under arrest?"

"Not yet." His frown lines creased deeper. "But if the autopsy confirms the poison, we'll get a search warrant first thing. And the guy's fingerprints are probably everywhere. Then we'll have something besides hunches to go on."

"But he's our minister," I said, feeling a quick wave of panic. I should have done more for him last night, but I couldn't think what. Pressed him a little harder to come up with other suspects, maybe, or helped him remember details that slipped his rattled mind. "He couldn't have killed her. It's against everything he stands for: *Thou shalt not kill.*"

"Unless you have a compelling motive," Meigs said with a shrug. "Say you want something badly and this Lacy Bailes is in your way. Then all bets are off." He moved around the desk and sat heavily, the seat cushion sighing with his weight.

"He's not like that," I insisted. "He's not

46

an angry man. Even when his wife left him . . . I could never picture him getting violent."

"Why did he insist that *you* be called last night?" Meigs asked.

I hesitated. "The deacons asked me to meet with him earlier in the fall, to make sure his personal issues weren't overwhelming him."

"And?"

"We chatted a bit and I gave him a referral. He seems to have righted his ship fairly quickly." None of his business that Wesley hadn't followed through and talked with Annabelle.

Meigs looked unconvinced. "Why did your former assistant pastor leave?"

"Excuse me?"

"The pastor the church is replacing — why did he leave?"

I shrugged. "No one expects to stay in that kind of position long. Most assistants get some experience and either decide parish ministry isn't for them or move on to a church of their own."

"So it was a normal progression in this particular case?"

I'd thought so. Reverend Leo was obviously ambitious. And Wesley wasn't going anywhere anytime soon. Though Leo had announced his change of plans rather abruptly. "He was hired to do youth work by a small church in New Hampshire. He seemed delighted with the opportunity."

"You mentioned that most churches select an interim minister while they're looking for a replacement." He glanced at his notes. "But yours determined an *intern* could do the job. Can you tell me more about that?"

I pressed back against the cold metal of the visitor's chair, feeling a little claustrophobic. "I don't remember exactly. I haven't been that involved with the church politics. I go when I can but . . ." I hunched my shoulders and laughed.

"On the other hand, Reverend Wesley chose you to take over Ms. Bailes's position. In your opinion, why didn't the church follow usual protocol?"

I rolled my head first to my right shoulder, and then to the left. "Like I said, I guess we figured we could muddle along with our divinity school intern helping out. We have a couple of retired ministers in the congregation who fill in from time to time. And we all assumed the search would go quickly, especially with Lacy Bailes at the helm — much faster than it has."

"And?"

"The committee has been very tight-lipped. Every week or two during the announcements, Lacy gets up" — I winced, using the present tense again — "got up and told us how well it was going. 'We've finished writing our church's profile to attract potential candidates. The applications are starting to come in. We're starting to visit candidates in their home territory.' That kind of thing. But if you went by their body language, none of the folks on the committee looked happy."

"So maybe it wasn't going as well as she suggested?"

I blinked and held my hands out. "I wasn't privy to the details. I'm just guessing."

"Do you remember who suggested there was no need for a temporary pastor?"

This man was a bulldog. "You'd have to go back and review the minutes of the council meeting to be sure. Probably Wesley made the suggestion and Reverend Leo supported it and everyone else fell in line." My heart hammered. Was everything I said going to implicate Wesley? "No one *really* likes the idea of an interim. It means getting used to one more person. And more time elapsed before the church gets back to normal."

I shifted in the chair. "You can compare it to taking time out after a divorce. A lot of people understand the idea of grieving their marriage, but most people push that aside and just dive into dating."

"Is that right?" He flashed a lopsided grin.

I felt heat seep across my face and neck.

"Is there anything else?" I asked, tapping my watch.

"So your assistant left abruptly, no interim was hired, and the search for a new padre has been delayed. Any other problems in your church lately?"

I crossed my arms over my chest and glared. "Maybe you should consider some suspects outside of our church. Maybe our Reverend Wesley Sandifer was just plain unlucky enough to find her, exactly the way he told you. I think you're wasting your time going down a dead-end alley."

"What else can you tell me about Ms. Bailes?"

"She was a recovering alcoholic. And a nice lady."

Meigs squared his shoulders and scratched a note on his pad. "Why did Mrs. Sandifer leave?"

I squirmed. "Just my opinion, nothing official?"

He waited, finally saying: "The stakes are high here. And you said he isn't your patient. You're not breaking his confidence."

"I doubt he'd see it that way," I said

sharply. "It's very important to him to look strong. He feels he can be a role model for handling grief and loss if he just carries on like normal."

"And you went along with that?"

"I tried to encourage him to try therapy without getting into a therapeutic relationship with him myself. It's not so easy to support someone when they don't let you in."

I took a deep breath, thinking suddenly of the detective's very sick wife. How was he hearing this? Should I ask him directly how she was doing? And what about *him?* It's so much easier to solve other people's thorny problems than to tackle your own.

"Why did she leave?" Meigs asked again. Impatiently.

"The truth is I don't know much. I imagine that the burden of being a minister's wife can be very heavy if you aren't prepared for it. In this case, she was expected to serve on the Women's League, the women's holiday fair, the outreach committee . . . the list goes on. Not that it was written in the bylaws or anything," I added, thinking that the congregation sounded needy and demanding. A subtle, steady, all-over weight, like wearing the dentist's X-ray apron for a lifetime. And Beverly wasn't even drawing a check. And she was married to fussy Wesley.

51

No wonder she split.

But how humiliating for him. How would he face counseling couples just embarking on the great sea of marriage, when his nuptial vessel had so recently sunk? I had to laugh. Mine had sunk too. And that didn't stop me from my daily rounds of psychotherapy nor my weekly advice column. Neither rain nor snow nor sleet nor hail, nor your own personal agita . . .

"In your opinion, who might have noticed if the reverend was having an affair?"

I stiffened, the image of Wesley with Lacy rushing back into my brain. "An affair? With whom? There was certainly nothing like that going on — certainly not with Lacy. Not that I was aware of."

"I'm not asking what you know. I'm asking who might know."

I shook my head slowly. "Jesus. This is bad." I sighed. "Nancy Wilcox. She's the church secretary. She sits right outside his office. She's his gatekeeper."

His eyebrows lifted. "Anyone else?"

"The sexton and his wife, Mr. and Mrs. McCabe. He works full-time and she's there a lot too. She cleans the offices and sits in for Nancy at lunchtime, days off, that kind of thing." My eyes fluttered shut. I felt exhausted and stupid. "Our Yale divinity student intern. He's around most days — he's one of the candidates for the associate pastor position. That's it for our regular staff. The financial people come for a few hours and leave as soon as they're finished. I can't see them having much insider information. Unless this is all about money?"

But what else didn't I know? I felt like a fool. I stood up and stamped the last clump of melting snow out of my boot tread. "If that's all you need then I have a pie in the oven."

Meigs glanced at his watch and grinned back up at me. I could guess what he was thinking: If I'd really left a baked good in my oven, it was a cinder by now.

CHAPTER 4

I dropped off a packet of Christmas cards at the post office and swung by Page Hardware for lightbulbs and birdseed for my deck feeder. By the time I got home, it was almost dark and starting to snow again, fat lazy flakes sure to cover the ice patches in a thin but treacherous layer.

Every unit in the condo complex was decked out with lights, wreathes, even one menorah — except for mine and Mrs. Dunbarton's. My security spotlights did not contribute much Christmas cheer. Even inside, I hadn't gotten any further with decorations than a bell-studded red velvet collar for Spencer. He jingled to greet me as I came in through the garage. The man in my life purrs and uses a litter box. Slightly pathetic.

Lately I've been beating back the early sunset blues. And telling myself the struggle is normal: Lots of people react badly to the truncated daylight even without a recent attempted kidnapping and a rocky family history.

Hands on hips, I stood in the entrance to the living room. Maybe it was time to get my own Christmas tree. This had been a point of contention in my marriage to Mark, who was Jewish — in the political sense. His father had survived the Holocaust in a concentration camp — not that anyone discussed this openly. But any time I mentioned Christmas decorations, he argued about the harm that'd been done by Christians to his people over the centuries. A connection I had to accept, even though he'd not set foot in a synagogue in the years I'd known him.

"Besides, it will be confusing to the children," he'd finally said.

I gaped at him. "What children?"

Another point of contention: Mark wasn't ready for that kind of responsibility. Never mind that he's forty years old and an associate professor of psychiatry at Yale. To be truthful, once you backed his neurosis out of the mix, it wasn't clear that I was ready either. When both your parents are gone by the time you're six — mother dead, father split — it's hard to resuscitate the image of a happy family. Just say the holidays are fraught with booby traps and landmines: old family baggage, the pressures of Currier and Ives expectations . . .

It'd taken so long for me to sort out the loose emotional ends of my short marriage; I hated to think what would happen ending a long marriage. The detective's face flashed to mind. He'd told me last September that he was about to ask for a divorce when his wife's diagnosis came. Now they were both faced with a life sentence, hers shorter than his.

I scooped up the purring cat, carried him into the bedroom, and dialed my sister's number. Brittany answered.

"Want to help your aunt pick out a Christmas tree?"

"Hooray!" she squealed and dropped the phone. "M-o-o-m-m! Aunt Rebecca's finally going to get a tree!"

I made arrangements to meet Janice at Tessa's Tree Farm the next afternoon. My good friend Angie called as soon as I hung up. She's smart, funny, and perennially upbeat, which allows me to forgive the tall, blond, and gorgeous part.

"What's new?" she asked.

I filled her in on the last twenty-four hours — the murder, the midnight ER visit to talk with Reverend Wesley, Detective Meigs's interest in my help.

"Sounds like he's interested in more than that," said Angie. "And I have to say I approve. You need to get away from the whiny intellectuals and find a real man's man."

"I'm not about to hover around this guy waiting for his wife to croak," I insisted, thinking the idea sounded slightly appealing, but unacceptably ruthless.

"Of course not, but it's no crime to be attractive, charming, and sympathetic about her illness. I'm telling you, divorcés and widowers do not last long in this market. If you'll get off your therapeutic high horse, you can help him grieve while you're dating."

"Not going to happen," I said firmly.

"Anyway, that's not why I called," she said. "An old friend from Princeton dropped in unexpectedly. He's visiting his parents in Old Saybrook."

"Another whiny intellectual?" I teased.

Angie ignored me. "I was hoping you could join us for dinner." She lowered her voice. "Not only is he a hunk, he's well-fixed. He got in on the bottom floor of the dot-com boom and bailed out at a good time too. Bothwell Bowser. He can't help the name — it's in the family. We call him Bob."

"Love to" — which I definitely wouldn't — "but I'm due at the church supper."

"What did you make?"

"Apple pie," I said without enthusiasm, knowing where this was headed.

"Count us in. If you two hit it off, we'll go for a nightcap after the Congregational crowd hits the hay."

I didn't even try to argue, just arranged to meet at the church at six.

Now my head was whirling with inappropriate thoughts about Detective Meigs, worry about Reverend Wesley, and sheer terror about meeting Angie's friend. I hadn't been on a date since the incident in September and very few before that. The idea of meeting a romantic prospect — even in a crowd at a church supper — was setting off a run of post-traumatic shock waves.

So I called up Dr. Aster. Enlisting her persona has a tranquilizing effect: She rarely takes a psychological misstep. And she always gets the last word. And it's gratifying to hear from readers who find her advice life-changing, sensible, or just plain funny. I skimmed through my readers' letters and settled on a problem that matched my mood and the season.

Dear Dr. Aster:

My husband and I have a lot of things in common but religion isn't one of them. I'm Catholic, he's Jewish — already we're arguing over the kids and I'm barely three months pregnant. It's very important to me to raise my children as Catholics. Not that I don't have my own issues with the church, but he seems to hate my religion. He suggests we expose the kids to both traditions — set up the Christmas tree and the menorah — and let them choose. I say that's teaching them to be nothing. Honestly, if we'd had this discussion before we got married, I'm not sure I would have gone through with it. Are we doomed?

Yours truly,
Trapped in Tacoma

Dear Trapped:
Oh pulleaze! If your husband hated your religion, would he be suggesting exposing his children to both his and yours?

Maybe it will help to realize you're not the first couple to be surprised

by this issue. With the specter of kids on the horizon, religious backgrounds that seemed quaint to a dating couple can easily develop into time bombs. The most important thing is to open the lines of communication — start by arranging conversations with both his rabbi and your priest. Many couples in your situation use the holidays as a joyful opportunity to teach the kids about their traditions.

Ugh. Many couples also use the holidays to support rampant materialism. So what. This was impossibly dull, and it didn't take a high-priced editor to point it out. Giving advice is harder when the issue hits close to home — like Jewish husbands for me. And probably divorce for Reverend Wesley. People expect us experts to be wise — to the point of inhuman. Not to mention funny. My Superwoman costume was at the dry cleaner's today.

I closed my advice column file and went online to check the *New Haven Register* for news about Lacy Bailes or poor nerdish Wesley. One way or another, the rumor mill would be grinding. How awful to have his dirty laundry aired so publicly. A minister is accustomed to a higher level of respect and admiration than the average fellow, but the price is life in a fishbowl.

POLICE INVESTIGATE WOMAN'S DEATH

GUILFORD — Lacy Bailes, 54, was taken to the Shoreline Emergency Clinic in Guilford where she died Friday night. Detective Jack Meigs confirmed that the death is under investigation.

A memorial service will be held on Tuesday at 11 a.m. at the Shoreline Congregational Church, with a private burial to follow.

Thank God there was nothing about Wesley. Yet.

I reconsidered Meigs's question about Reverend Leo's quick departure. I'd started attending the church after Mark moved out, a couple months before Leo made his exit. Leo resembled his namesake — curly blond hair and a full mustache. He was attractive, gregarious, and outgoing, the polar opposite of Reverend Wesley. Some ministers are extroverts, while others are good one-on-one but despise the social jungle that is the post-service coffee hour. Leo was a natural

61

— the kind of guy who stood at the door and made children and elderly women giggle by holding his hand out: "Tickets, please."

In fact, Leo and Wesley had made a good pair. They worked out a Sunday routine: Leo pressed the flesh and Wesley retreated to his office to check on the treasurer and the church's financials. Wesley simply isn't a natural crowd pleaser, though he does well with the hospitalized and the dying. He gets excited talking about church projects and he doesn't mind sitting quietly — sometimes that's all it takes. Sometimes the proverbial blind pig finds an acorn: He comes out of a visit with a whopping contribution to the building fund or the youth mission trip to rural Maine. In the end, he might have gone into the wrong business altogether. I wondered if he thought that too.

Looking back, I could see the church had been in a bit of a funk since Leo left. Attendance was lower — including mine — and so was morale. I chewed on another one of Meigs's questions: Why had we really dispensed with an interim assistant minister? Leo was just the kind of man who would be missed terribly and whose footsteps would be hard to follow.

I carried the pie out to the car, cranked

the heater to max, and drove slowly downtown, too nervous to appreciate the lit and decorated tree on the town green. How quickly could I summon up a case of the stomach flu or viral pneumonia? A blind date at a church supper? Huge mistake. I imagined how our church hall might look through a sophisticated stranger's eyes: the painted cement-block walls, the green plastic "tablecloths" stretched over industrial tables, the handmade decorations, the thrift-store silverware, and the Women's League members dressed in reindeer horns and Christmas-themed aprons. On the plus side, the whole nightmare, and me with it, should be put to bed by nine p.m.

Angie was knocking the snow off her boots just inside the church house door when I arrived.

"Rebecca Butterman, meet Bob Bowser." She grabbed my mittened hand and pressed it into the paw of a towering black-haired man with soulful brown eyes that — so help me — reminded me of Mrs. Meigs's. He looked perfect next to Angie, who tops out around six feet. I felt like a pygmy in comparison, like neighbor Babette Finster's mini dog, Wilson, yapping at their ankles.

I deposited my pie on the dessert table and buzzed around the room looking for seats where our tablemates would neither drive the dark god directly out into the cold night nor listen in and later repeat every awkward conversational foray to the rest of the congregation. A back corner table had three unclaimed spots, next to two folding chairs marked as "taken" with coats. I parked Angie's purse and my purse and scarf on the empty seats, and started toward the buffet, which groaned with homemade casseroles and salads. Paul Cashman, the Yale Divinity School intern, gripped my forearm.

"Can I speak to you for a minute?" His usually tidy hair was flattened except for the swirling tufts of a cowlick.

"Go on ahead," I told Angie and Bob. "I'll be right along."

Paul looked bleached out and worried, high-wire tense; not at all his usual humble and calm persona.

"Did you hear about Lacy?" I asked.

"Awful," Paul said, swallowing several times quickly. He pulled on his tie — turning bright red when he realized the tip had caught in his fly. "I feel sick about it."

I looked away to give him a moment to adjust his clothing and nodded, tongue clucking.

"Reverend Wesley says you'll take the

empty chair on the search committee," Paul continued.

"You've talked to Wesley? How is he?"

"I drove him home from the clinic this morning," Paul said. "He's resting comfortably."

I took that to mean drugged to the gills.

"Will you take the position?" he asked again. "We really need you."

"Of course," I said, patting the knotted muscles of his skinny shoulder. "I'm happy to help."

He whooshed out a breath. "Thank God. Don't let me keep you from your friends."

Before I could ask if Paul had learned anything more about Lacy's death, a skinny photographer dragged him away to pose with a pair of screaming children with nasty head colds. And Santa: Mr. McCabe dressed in faded red felt and a ratty white beard.

Why was *Paul* so eager to have me on the committee? Had I given the impression that I'd support him as our assistant? Not that I wouldn't. But to do the job right, besides oiling the troubled waters, I had every intention of listening to each candidate and then giving the committee my honest feedback.

When I reached the buffet, Angie and Bob had moved past the salads and were tunneling into the casseroles. I fell into line, picked up a Corel plate, and slunk by a dish labeled in shaky handwriting as Mrs. Wiggett's traditional Christmas mold — green Jell-O shot through with maraschino cherries and mini marshmallows. Mrs. Wiggett herself, reindeer antlers askew, pushed a large serving spoon across the table.

"You won't want to miss my mold," she said. I thought I detected a whiff of alcohol. No drinking is allowed on the church premises — we have three hundred years of Puritanism to live up to. But that doesn't keep folks from tippling before they arrive.

"It came out perfectly this year," added Mrs. McCabe, the sexton's wife. She was swathed in a green corduroy jumper that matched the Jell-O, antlers perched on her thick brown hair, and red lightbulbs hanging from her earlobes and flashing in mesmerizing cadence. "Isn't it awful about Lacy? We are all so distraught."

"Unbelievable." I shook my head, trying to remember if I'd put her name on the detective's list of church insiders. I carved out a token blob of Jell-O. "Have you spoken with Reverend Wesley today?"

"Remember, you're not on the case," a hoarse voice whispered.

The serving spoon dropped out of my fingers and clattered to the floor — Detective Meigs stood behind me. I squatted down, retrieved the spoon, and turned to face him, hoping I hadn't turned as red as Paul. Wiping the spoon with my paper napkin, I slid it back onto the table.

"What are *you* doing here?"

He hefted his plate, loaded with meat loaf, fried chicken, and scalloped potatoes. "The sandwich board on the town green said supper was open to the public. I assumed that included me." He leaned in close and added under his breath, "I'd like to try to blend in a bit. Mind if I sit with you?"

"I'm here with a date," I stammered.

"I'd love to meet him," Meigs said, smiling wolfishly.

"There are only three open seats," I said.

"I can squeeze in."

"Fine." I added a scoop of macaroni and cheese next to the mashed potatoes and doused them both with gravy. "Follow me."

I wound my way through the green-clad tables, dotted with red napkins, plastic snowmen, and mini poinsettias, Meigs in my wake. Angie's eyes bugged wide when she saw him.

"Angie, Bob, this is Detective Jack Meigs," I said in a low voice. "He's with the cops."

Meigs nodded at Angie. "Didn't we meet earlier this fall?" Then he reached over to

67

wring Bob's hand. Bob was taller but Meigs quite possibly had fifty pounds on him, most of it gristle.

He pulled out one of the coat-draped seats.

"That one's taken," I said.

"Let me get another chair," Bob said, unfurling his six-foot-plus frame gracefully.

"He can get it himself," I said. But Bob had already crossed the room to a stack of metal chairs that leaned against the wall. Meigs took Bob's seat.

"Do you belong to this church?" Angie asked.

"Lapsed Catholic. But the food looks better here." Meigs winked, tucked a red napkin under his chin, and shoveled up a forkful of meat loaf.

"Grace first," I hissed.

He replaced the fork on his plate and grinned. Bob returned, snapped open the folding chair, and squeezed in on the other side of me. Paul Cashman climbed the steps to the stage at our end of the room.

He gripped a handheld microphone and flapped his arms like a startled goose. "Merry Christmas!" His forced smile faded. "I'm sorry we have to start out on a sad note, but I know we all hold the family of Lacy Bailes in our prayers." The dinner guests buzzed as he squeezed his eyes shut and blinked them open. The few who hadn't already heard the news about Lacy's suspicious death were now getting it from their neighbors. "The fellowship committee suggested we sing the first verse of 'Joy to the World' before dinner," he said.

He pointed at the pianist and broke into song, half a beat ahead and half an octave higher than was comfortable for my limited alto range. I hated myself for feeling embarrassed, but it seemed so corny, singing in front of the men. Though Bob was warbling happily, even tilting his head and shifting to a descant echo when we reached "heaven and nature sing." Only Meigs stood with his arms crossed and eyes squinting as he cased the roomful of singers. He wanted to blend in? What a bust.

"May we join our hearts together for a blessing?" Paul asked after the pianist's final flourish.

Mrs. Wiggett and Mrs. McCabe appeared at our table, deposited their plates in front of the reserved chairs, and clasped hands. Without looking to either side, I slid my hand into Meigs's leathery palm on the left, and Bob's smooth one on the right. I closed my eyes, sweat prickling my upper lip. Under my breath, I whispered my own small-minded prayer. "Please Lord don't let my hands get slippery."

"Gracious God, we thank you for the gift of your Son and the celebration of the Christmas season. Be with Lacy Bailes's family in this time of sorrow. Amen."

I blinked my eyes open in time to see Paul slap the mike into its stand and bolt off the stage.

"What's with him?" Meigs muttered, still gripping my hand. I felt the thick callus on his palm as I extracted my fingers and reached for a napkin to pat my upper lip.

"That's our Yale intern," I said. "He's upset tonight" — I stared at Meigs — "and it makes perfect sense. With Wesley under the weather, he's suddenly got a lot more responsibility than he bargained for. It's not so easy to balance Christmas joy with death."

I noticed Mrs. McCabe craning to hear our conversation. "Such a nice young man," she said. "He's only been here a couple of months and he's so organized and poised. I'm very impressed with him."

"Nice enough," said Mrs. Wiggett, her chin pushed out to a strong *V.* She rotated her plate and spooned into her Jell-O. "But I'm concerned that with a little stress, he's already coming undone."

The mashed potatoes I was chewing suddenly tasted like sawdust.

"He does the job more than competently," said Mrs. McCabe. "Besides" — she began to hum — "he's a hunka hunka burnin' love." Then, as she noticed the two people who approached our table, I swear she said, "Oh shit."

Skinny, pale Paul Cashman, a hunka hunka burnin' love? Had she been drinking too?

Barney Brooks, a tall, distinguished man with white hair and a closely cropped white beard, cleared his throat. He straightened his tie, navy blue and dotted with little golfing Santas.

"I'd like you all to meet the Reverend Ellen Dark. She's visiting us from New Hampshire this weekend just to get a feel for the area. Our committee will be interviewing her tomorrow night." He glowered at Mrs. Wiggett and then directed a businesslike smile at me. "We hope five o'clock suits your schedule. And we'll have a short meeting for committee members only right after church."

"That's fine," I said. "Whatever it takes." I stood and shook Ellen Dark's hand. Her sea gray eyes twinkled and she held on several seconds too long.

"It's so lovely to be here at this time of year. My husband and I have made a little vacation out of the week. In this business, you learn to grab your relaxation when you can. A minister is always on," she explained to no one in particular. "Every conversation can turn into a pastoral counseling session. So it's important to get away and attend to your own self-care. My, my, the ladies in your church sure can cook." She patted her thickened middle. "I would miss the New Hampshire cuisine but no worry about wasting away to nothing here!"

"Do you hear a buzzing noise?" Meigs whispered. I stifled a laugh.

"I'm so very sorry about Miss Bailes," said Ellen. "She was a formidable woman and I know her passing has torn a hole in your church fabric. But I'm sure you feel that way about Reverend Leo too. Change is so hard, but isn't that just life?"

Barney Brooks broke in to wish us good night, grasped Reverend Dark's elbow, and began to propel her to the next table.

"There's a woman who could talk a dog off a meat wagon," said Angie.

Bob laid his fork on his plate, wiped his lips with his paper napkin, and turned to me. "Angie tells me you're a psychologist. My favorite sister is too." His smile lines crinkled in an appealing way.

"What kind of work does she do?" I asked.

"She works in the health-care center at Williams College," he said. "Most of her patients are students."

"I love working with students," I said. "They have so much potential for change. I help with the Yale peer counselor program. Which isn't to say —"

"I think I'll take my dessert on the road," said Meigs loudly. "Will you walk me out?"

Angie rolled her eyes. She'd been in favor of me chasing after him in theory, but apparently not when pitted against her friend Bob. Or was she objecting to Meigs's imperiousness? I didn't find it all that attractive.

"Please excuse me?" I asked Bob. "I'm sorry to interrupt. I'll be right back."

I glared at Meigs as we both got to our feet, and glowered at his back as he wove through the tables of chattering diners. He stopped at the dessert buffet long enough to scoop a selection of Christmas cookies into a napkin.

He strode into the long corridor and turned to face me. "Call me tomorrow after the meeting," he said, rubbing his eye, leaving a trail of green sparkles on his forehead. "And after the interview too. Pay close attention to both Cashman and Dark. See if

73

you can get a sense of what Ms. Bailes thought of each of them, without asking directly. Do you understand what I'm saying? I just want your observations. I'll draw the conclusions."

I was stunned, then annoyed.

"Why not record the meeting and leave me out of it altogether?"

"Don't be so touchy." Meigs laughed and chucked my chin, which I detest even in the best of circumstances.

"No one in this church would kill anyone else. Maybe you'd better focus your cracker-jack detective skills on some other line of thinking."

"Is that so?" He grinned, tucked a folded wad of paper into my purse, and lumbered out.

I whirled away and stomped off to the ladies' room. What an oaf. The kind moment we'd shared in the cemetery a couple months ago must have been an aberration. I was going directly back to the table and asking well-mannered Bob out for a drink.

On my way out of the bathroom, I heard a loud noise in the stairwell, then a series of thumps. I sprinted over and flung open the double doors. My feet shot out from under me. I tumbled half a flight down, crashing onto a body crumpled on the landing.

"Detective Meigs! Jack! Help!" I screamed.

CHAPTER 5

The man underneath me groaned. My
cheek was pressed close to his, near enough
to catch the marriage of coffee and garlic
on his breath. His elbow was jammed into
my stomach. I shifted away and winced with
pain. Had I broken my leg? And he'd taken
a worse fall than me from the sound of it,
crashing down half a flight of stairs and
landing without a human cushion.

I rolled off of him gingerly, able to make
out Paul Cashman's pale face in the dim
light. His eyes were closed. "Paul? Paul, are
you all right?" I touched his shoulder.

He groaned again but said nothing. I
remembered my phone, wedged in the back
pocket of my slacks. I wiggled it out, clicked
to incoming calls, and punched redial. The
last call I'd gotten had been from Meigs.
The phone rang three times, then his voicemail picked up, unwelcoming and gruff.

"You've reached Detective Meigs. Leave a

message or if this is an emergency, dial 911 for the police headquarters." Jesus, wasn't he supposed to *be* the cops?

"Paul?" No response now, not a flicker. As my eyes adjusted to the dark stairwell, I could see the blood oozing from his forehead and pooling in his ear. He seemed to have slammed his head into the radiator on the landing. I tried to push off to my feet but my ankle buckled, bringing sharp pain and tears. I stabbed at the phone — 911 — the hell with Meigs.

"There's been an accident," I said, my voice shrill. "We're in the east stairwell of the Shoreline Congregational Church — the fellowship building. The stairs that lead to the basement. A man has a head injury. And my leg hurts," I added, suppressing a sob.

"Don't move him," the woman who answered the phone barked. She confirmed the church's address. "If you have a blanket available, keep him warm. And stay on the line, we'll get someone out to you as soon as we can."

I wiggled out of my sweater and tucked it around Paul's shoulders. It suddenly occurred to me that Angie was in the building. "I'll call you back," I told the dispatcher. Then I dialed Angie's cell phone, bursting into tears when she answered.

"We'll be right there," she yelped when I finished explaining.

Just a minute later, footsteps pounded in the hallway above me. The doors swung open and Mrs. McCabe popped her head in, allowing a beam of light from the hallway to illuminate Paul's ashen face. She screamed. "Oh my God, what happened?"

"Be careful," I yelled up. "Don't come any closer. There's something slippery at the top of the stairs. Call the sexton to get the lights."

The fluorescent fixtures flickered on at the same time that Paul's eyes opened and met mine. "Reverend Wesley is going —" He lapsed back into unresponsiveness.

"Going where?" I whispered, touching my hand to his cheek.

Mrs. McCabe returned to the hall with her husband. They crab-walked across the slippery linoleum to the railing and peered down the stairwell.

"Be careful," I called again. The sexton knelt to run his hand over the gray speckled flooring leading to the top step.

"For the love of God, it looks like Crisco if it looks like anything," Mr. McCabe exclaimed, holding up two fingers. "What in the *H E* double *L* is this doing here?"

Angie and Bob burst through the door

behind the McCabes. "Rebecca, are you okay?"

"Step aside, stand back, please," a loud voice ordered.

"That's my friend," Angie insisted, her head bobbing above the gathering crowd of supper attendees. "She's been injured. I'm going down."

"Stay where you are."

A chunky Guilford policeman with a bulbous, reddened nose pushed past Angie and spread his arms to prevent anyone from coming down the stairs. "Is the man breathing?" he called down to me.

I held my palm an inch from Paul's nostrils. "Yes."

A thin cop materialized next to the big guy and squatted to study the opaque paste smeared across the linoleum. "Should I go down this way?" he asked.

"Ambulance is here," piped up a reedy voice from the hallway.

"You people stay put now. Is there another way in?" barked the fat cop. All he needed was a Santa suit and a better attitude.

"I'll show you," said the sexton. "There's an emergency exit in the basement."

Minutes later, I heard the door open below and the crash of equipment and hurried footsteps. I inched into the corner away from Paul to make room. Two paramedics, trailed by the small policeman, maneuvered a stretcher up the stairs, packed Paul onto it, and whisked him out. The policeman turned to me.

"Now it's your turn, little lady."

"I'm fine," I said.

The paramedics returned with an empty gurney.

"Dispatcher said your leg was broken."

"I'm sure the ankle's just twisted," I said, smiling weakly. "No need to bother with me."

"Get on the damn stretcher," Angie shouted from upstairs. "They have to check you out and you're holding up Paul. Bob and I will meet you at the clinic."

Outside the church house, snow was whipping through the parking lot, swirling into tall eddies — a "dusting" had been forecast. I closed my eyes while my stretcher was rattled into the back of the ambulance, an arm's length from Paul. He was belted in tightly, mumbling through the oxygen mask strapped over his nose and mouth. I reached over to take his hand. *Peace in this season,* I prayed. It wasn't going well so far.

After I had my right leg palpated by a harried young doctor, then X-rayed, and then wrapped, the two policemen interviewed me about the stairwell incident. Angie and Bob hovered just outside the examining room door.

"You heard a noise then fell down the stairs onto Mr. Cashman," said the thin cop after checking the notes on his Palm Pilot. His pants drooped with the weight of his gun belt.

"I didn't *fall* exactly," I said. "I slid on the gunk and pitched forward. Paul must have slipped on the same stuff."

"That crap didn't get there by mistake," said Angie from the hallway. "It wasn't an accident. Didn't you see — it was spread all the way across the step like icing on a cake."

"Death by shortening," said the Santa cop with a sour chuckle. "That's a new one on me."

I wanted to deck him.

"Any ideas about who would have done something like this?" the thin cop asked me.

"Not really," I said. "No one would have known I was going down those stairs. I only went because I heard the noise when Paul Cashman fell."

The cops exchanged a look. "Where was Mr. Cashman going?" asked the heavyset cop.

"His office is in the basement — he's our

81

intern. Hardly anyone else uses that stairway." I pulled my coat around my shoulders, suddenly chilled. "How's he doing?"

The thin cop shrugged. "He's being transferred to Yale overnight for observation. They think it's a concussion, probably nothing worse," he said. "He'll have one hell of a headache in the morning, that's all."

"Thank you," I said, shivering. Bob laid a comforting hand on my shoulder.

A nurse in pale green scrubs bustled into the room carrying paperwork and a computer disk. "Doctor says no break. Just a minor sprain." *Minor* said with special emphasis. "Keep it elevated and iced, fifteen minutes on, fifteen off. Your X-ray is here" — she held up the disk — "any problems you can take this to your own doctor." She handed me a packet of Advil and a pair of crutches.

"You nearly break your leg and they offer you Advil?" Angie asked as I pushed myself up to standing.

"Don't be silly." I arranged the crutches, took a tentative step, and winced.

Bob came forward to support my elbow. "No dancing tonight," he said. I had to smile.

I limped with him down the hall, stopping to rest halfway across the reception area.

Near a Norfolk pine tree draped in white lights beside the exit, a large man squatted by a small woman in a wheelchair. Her wrists were tiny and her face and neck were chalky; a blue vein pulsed at her temple. The man leaned forward, resting his large, square hands on her lap, and spoke in a low voice. She nodded once and took a shallow breath. She had black hair and brown eyes almost as dark — Meigs's wife, of course. He looked up and caught my eye, slowly straightening, his hands dropping to his sides.

"Are you all right?" he asked. "I heard about the accident on the scanner."

"Fine," I said, lifting my chin in his wife's direction.

"I'm sorry I didn't get back to you. Alice was having trouble breathing."

"He insisted we come," the woman said, stretching to squeeze Meigs's fingers tenderly, then pull them to her cheek. "He looks like a bear but he's really such a softie." She tilted her head and smiled.

"I'm Dr. Butterman," I said, hobbling over to offer a handshake. Her hand felt like a baby bird out of the nest too soon. "Rebecca. The detective — your husband — helped me with a case last fall."

"Nice to meet you. I'm Alice." She adjusted the crocheted afghan across her legs, alternating squares of maroon and pink. "Jack doesn't like to bring his work home and that's fine with me, as you might imagine. You're a doctor?"

"Shrink," the detective said. "Head-shrinker."

"I wonder if she could do anything with you?" Alice peered up at him, her chuckle suddenly strangled into a rasping breath.

"I'll take you home," Meigs said, tucking the blanket around her and wheeling her toward the door. "Good night," he called over his shoulder.

I limped out behind them with my friends.

Angie and I waited under the portico for Bob to get the car. "I was wrong," she said. "Forget about the casserole and move on. Bob's great, don't you think?"

I pinched my lips together, feeling a little sick. I hadn't misheard Meigs last fall saying he had planned to ask for a divorce just before Alice was diagnosed — I was sure about that. But if they still had those kinds of problems, they hid them well in public.

Chapter 6

Spencer woke me the next morning walking across my chest and yowling for breakfast. I rolled over to look at the clock; the bright light slanting through the blinds stabbed my brain. Nine ten. I never sleep so late. But after Angie and Bob had driven me home from the emergency clinic, they'd come in for scotch and chocolate-chip cookies. I was too shaken up about Paul's close call — and mine — to be left alone.

"Your church crowd seems to have bad Karma," Angie had said. "Or there's some part of 'love your neighbor as yourself' that someone doesn't get."

"First of all, they're not my crowd," I said irritably. "And second, no one's out to hurt anyone else in that church."

Angie's eyebrows rose delicately. She's an atheist who believes more harm's been done in the name of religion than good. I say any organization where humans are involved can be twisted to evil. And I appreciate having reminders about leading a good life. To me a sermon is something like an advice column — comforting the sick at heart and counseling the confused. Take it or leave it, but at least listen. It might spark a good idea.

"So the Crisco was just a case of sloppy housekeeping?"

"I have no earthly clue." I scrabbled through my purse for a ChapStick and came across the papers Meigs had shoved into the front pocket. "What the hell?" It was a brochure describing the Women's League: history and purpose, budget, committee chairs, programs planned for the year. I'd been the featured speaker in November, talking about Dr. Aster's advice, especially handling holiday stress. My eye caught on the topic for December. The "Poison Lady" had visited to discuss common domestic problems — poisonous plants, dangerous cleaning products, hidden household killers. The description promised that the talk would be spiced up with illustrations from famous poisonings, real and fictional.

"Good gawd," I said, pushing the pamphlet across the coffee table. "No wonder he thinks one of us did it."

Angie wrinkled her nose. "Who thinks one

of you did it?"

"Meigs," I said, my voice tightening. "He must have found this at the church supper."

"That guy could use a charm school refresher," Bob said with a grin.

Angie skimmed the paper. "If the police have this information, there's no need for you to think about it for one more minute," she said. "Let's have that nightcap." She settled me on the couch and went to pour.

Halfway through a double Dewar's, Angie bustled out, not-so-subtly claiming fatigue and an early morning yoga class. Bob stayed, and we talked about his sister's interest in therapy, his recent hiking excursion through the Cotswolds, and finally, my shock about slipping on the linoleum and somersaulting down the stairs onto Paul.

"My whole life's felt like that lately," I admitted. "The divorce" — I checked to see if he looked shocked; he didn't — "moving here, and then . . ." I narrowed my eyes. "I suppose Angie told you what happened in September?"

"She said you'd come close to being raped. I'm so sorry." He reached for my hand, brown eyes warm with sympathy. "My sister would say an event like tonight can stir those feelings right up again." He laughed, squeezed my hand, and returned it to my knee. "May as well be honest: My own shrink's reminded me of that a time or two. It's not very macho to admit you've been in therapy, is it?"

"Totally refreshing," I said, leaning back into the cushions. I started to tuck my legs under me, then grimaced, feeling a twinge in my ankle. "Depending, of course, on what your presenting problem was."

He laughed. "Nothing very dramatic. Post-divorce stress. How's that leg? Shall I get the ice pack?"

I briefly considered the urge to snuggle, then stood up clutching my glass. "Thanks, I'm fine." I hobbled to the kitchen and poured the last inch of liquor down the sink.

"Bedtime for Bonzos," I told Bob. I liked him just fine, but if anything developed between us, it was going to happen slowly. Not the result of a woozy miscalculation. Not because he happened along when an accident left me exhausted and vulnerable. And to be honest, a little hollow about Detective Jack Meigs.

I rolled out of bed and limped into the kitchen to start coffee. I'd have to hustle to get to church. Staying in bed sounded mighty appealing but I had a feeling the search committee abhorred a vacuum. If I didn't show, Mrs. Wiggett or, worse still, Barney Brooks would puff up to fill the missing chair.

I turned on the shower and popped two more Advil. All things considered, my ankle didn't feel as bad as I expected — I wouldn't need those crutches. With a stream of hot water loosening the knots in my back, I mulled over last night's catastrophe. I was absolutely certain that my fall had been an accident of unlucky timing. But not Paul's. As I'd told the cops, Paul is the only staff person with an office in the basement. And he tends to hold his counseling sessions and meetings in the first-floor conference room.

"Hideous enough that a member has to talk with the intern," Paul joked just last week, "never mind going to Hell to do it."

Meaning someone who knows the church routine also knows that Paul could be expected to go up and down those stairs, but rarely anyone else. Occasionally Mr. McCabe goes down to fetch cleaning supplies or check on the furnace, but in my mind, the intended victim had to be Paul. But why hurt Paul? And why use such a — how else to put it — stupid method?

Angie told me last night that she'd watched the Guilford police map the edges of the swath of Crisco with a flashlight. It was wide enough that the perpetrator would have needed to layer on the grease, then retreat down the stairs and out the basement door. Or, start from the stairs and work back to the double doors and move out into the hall, where they'd stand a good chance of being spotted by one of the church-supper diners.

Once dressed, I wrapped my ankle in an Ace bandage for good measure, filled a travel mug with coffee, and set off to church. By the time I slid into a back pew, the last bars of the organ's opening sonata were fading. Reverend Chanton, a retired minister who fills in when the Lord and our ministers call him, stood to welcome the congregants. With his gaunt frame and sepulchral voice, he cut a somewhat cadaverous figure. The first half hour of the service dragged, gloomy in spite of the lighting of the Advent candle symbolizing joy and our preschool choir squeaking through "Away in a Manger."

"And now we take a time to share our congregational joys and concerns," Reverend Chanton intoned. "As always, we pray for our president, our governor, our first selectman, and all those in leadership positions. We think of those serving in our armed forces, especially Michael Dodge, Lorrie and Eric Petersen's son-in-law in

Iraq. We pray for Paul Cashman, who fell and suffered a head injury during the church supper last night."

The sexton had been creeping up the side aisle as Reverend Chanton talked. Now he darted over to the podium and passed him a note. The minister adjusted his reading glasses, plowed his throat clear, and read.

"Paul is improving rapidly and expected home later tonight. He thanks you for your kind wishes, but asks that you hold your visits and casseroles." He glanced up, smiled, and returned his gaze to his own paper. "We offer prayers for our Reverend Wesley, diagnosed with whooping cough. We hold Lacy Bailes and her family in our prayers."

The buzz that had started with the announcement about Paul picked up in volume and intensity. "The funeral is planned for Tuesday at eleven with a reception to follow. Anyone interested in providing baked goods or finger sandwiches should contact Beth Abbott during coffee hour."

I slipped out two-thirds of the way through the sermon — impossible to concentrate with the coffee I'd mainlined pressing on my bladder. Besides, I couldn't keep my mind off the trap that had been set for Paul. And wonder whether the Poison Lady had unintentionally provided a murder weapon to Lacy's killer.

I limped to the ladies' room and then over to the fellowship hall for a cup of tea and another Advil. My foot throbbed and I felt the first scratchy warning signals of a sore throat. The state of Connecticut probably hadn't seen whooping cough in forty years, and wouldn't you know the first case shows up in our congregation. If Reverend Wesley had passed me these germs on top of everything else . . .

The burbling coffeemaker was loud in the empty hall. My stomach rumbled at the sight of a basket of donut holes, two homemade coffee cakes, and several pies left over from the previous night's supper, all wrapped in Saran. I nibbled a piece of crust that had fallen to the table. It was oilier than mine, but with a nice flaky texture. The Women's League doesn't use my recipe — they prefer solid shortening. *Crisco.*

Had the cops followed up on the gunk spread across the stairs? And more to the point, was Crisco a staple in our church kitchen?

I poked my head into the kitchen. Deserted. Moving as quickly and quietly as my sore ankle allowed, I crossed the room and opened the doors of the wooden cupboard nearest the sexton's office. I found sugar, Maxwell House, a box of Tetley tea that might have dated from the 1950s, and three ancient canisters of salt. Behind the other items were two cans of Crisco. I tore a paper towel off the roll hanging on the wall, lifted out the first container, and pried it open, careful not to touch the can or its plastic lid. The seal inside hadn't been broken. I returned the can to the cupboard, lifted out the second can, and pulled off the lid.

This shortening was half gone, the reverse image of someone's scooping fingers imprinted in the white grease. Was this the grease in question? Who would know where to find our lard? Who would even *think* of using Crisco? And for what reason? *Don't jump to conclusions. Meigs wants data, not opinions.*

I flashed on the tender moment I'd witnessed the night before between Meigs and his wife. Embarrassing to be so transparent: Even a neophyte shrink could see I was avoiding the challenges and hazards of looking for a new man by feeding fantasies of Meigs, who was altogether inappropriate and inaccessible. What had gone wrong with their marriage before Alice got sick? I pinched my thigh. Time to move on.

"Rebecca?" Footsteps slapped in the

hallway and Mrs. Wiggett's voice trilled. "Have you seen Rebecca Butterman?"

A man's voice answered. "No."

"If you see her, would you tell her we're meeting in the parlor?"

I quickly fitted the lid back onto the Crisco. I couldn't very well carry the can into the meeting. Not a good idea to leave it here either. What if it turned out to be important evidence and the person responsible came back for it before I could tell the cops?

Using paper towels like pot holders, I carried the can across the room and buried it deep at the bottom of a box full of cardboard coffee cups.

Let Meigs decide the rest.

CHAPTER 7

As I exited the kitchen, I noticed an orange traffic cone had been placed in the hall, the kind the sexton uses to reserve a parking space when someone's loading food for the soup kitchen. This time the cone blocked the stairs where Paul and I had fallen the night before.

I walked across the hall to the meeting. Our parlor can be lit either by stand-alone tag-sale lamps with low-watt bulbs and hideous gold and brown swirl lampshades or eye-glazing overhead fluorescents. The committee had opted for dim, except for the spotlight on the dark oil portrait of the Reverend Franklin Bower in his dress black robe. His disapproving gaze seemed to follow me as I came into the room.

Barney Brooks and Mrs. Wiggett were settled into upholstered chairs patterned in pink scallops. I was astonished to see my neighbor, Babette Finster, who had almost disappeared into the deep pocket of the striped wing chair, leaving the backbreaking, sleigh-bed fainting couch for me. Babette was on the committee?

I guess I hadn't paid much attention to the group's composition. To be honest, I'd missed more Sunday mornings lately than I'd made. Somehow, just as in the aftermath of 9/11, when attendance had surged, church had seemed more urgent in the first lonely days of my separation and divorce — my personal terrorist attack. Now that I was feeling less scared and more settled, a bit of apathy had settled in too. But surely Babette would have mentioned the committee when we met on one of her early morning loops with Wilson? Although she'd been more anxious than ever since the incident in September — hardly able to stick to one line of conversation.

"Babette. I didn't realize you were working on the search." I hoped my smile was encouraging, not critical.

"I was an alternate. When Frank dropped out with his back surgery, they brought me in." Babette pressed her lips together, quivering, face white. "They said everything is confidential."

"For God's sake, Babette, you're allowed to say you're a member," said Barney

Brooks. "We're supposed to give the impression that we're approachable and responsive."

Mrs. Wiggett waved her hand. "Let's get down to business. We're in a terrible position here."

I signaled *T* for time-out. As I remind my Yale peer counselors, feelings first, solutions second. "Do you think it would be helpful to talk a little about Lacy's death? It's all been such a horrible shock."

Babette nodded. "On Thursday, she was alive, sitting exactly where you're sitting." She pointed a shaking finger at me, pale blue eyes bright with unshed tears. "And then she was poisoned."

"We don't know that for sure," I said. "There's going to be an autopsy."

"She was a dynamic woman," said Barney Brooks with a tight smile. "I understand she ran a very big department in her company. We tried to overlook it when she got pushy. Maybe someone at work took offense at her techniques."

"Don't be absurd," said Mrs. Wiggett, her own expression growing pinched. "You don't poison someone for being bossy. She meant the best. And being in charge was so important to her. She didn't have anyone at home. Mr. Wiggett may have his flaws but I do feel safer with him in his lounge chair."

Babette shuddered and wrapped her arms around her thin torso. I doubted that her little Wilson provided the same sense of security as the basking and substantial Mr. Wiggett. Neither did Spencer, though a warm, furry feline body is definitely better than nothing.

"Best thing this committee can do to honor Lacy is get to work," said Barney. "She wouldn't want a big consciousness-raising session. She wasn't that kind of woman."

"Agreed," said Mrs. Wiggett. "We don't have time to waste either. Lacy offered to gather all the references. Do you know anything about that?" she asked me.

"She took notes at every meeting," Babette said. She twisted her pearl earring, eyes darting around the circle. "We should probably have done more but she was so good at it."

"I'm the one who set up the interviews," Barney said, huffing. "She was supposed to report at this meeting about the phone calls," he told me. "So we'd all be on the same page by the time our candidates came in."

"If only we could get into her files to

check," said Babette, looking close to melt-down.

"Maybe she left a copy of her notes in the church office. But let's start at the beginning," I suggested. Time to dust off that famous soothing psychological presence. "Tell me what you've done so far. And then we can figure out what's missing and how to proceed."

"Central office sent us dozens of applications," said Barney Brooks. "We read through all of them. There weren't many candidates we liked. As you know, we're interviewing Paul tomorrow — if he feels well enough — and Ellen Dark this evening."

"Lacy didn't seem to care for either one of them," sniffed Mrs. Wiggett. "She wanted us to keep looking. Always a mistake to rush an important decision — that's what she told us." She frowned, the pleats of skin under her chin trembling. "As if we hadn't already spent hours and hours on this process."

"And how do you feel about the options?" I asked.

"Paul is a fine young man," she said. "Reverend Wesley certainly favors him. But it's not right to be badgered into choosing based on his preferences."

Barney straightened his tie, grasped the arms of his chair, and leaned forward, his white beard bristling. "We need maturity, not untested ideas that will tear us apart. We don't need a young single man who will put thoughts in our girls' heads. We already have a man at the helm — we have Wesley. We need a woman's touch in this position."

"Do you remember which references Lacy was planning to call?" I asked.

All three rustled uncomfortably. "Maybe Paul's adviser at the Yale Divinity School?" Babette ventured.

"Do you have his or her name?" I asked.

"Lacy kept the notes," repeated Babette. "I offered to act as secretary but she said it was easier to do it herself. She said she'd email everything to us."

Four committee members and only one had written things down? Lacy had clearly ruled them with an iron hand. Odd, because two out of three weren't pushovers. Maybe a budding case of learned helplessness: Lacy's ongoing rejection of their efforts led them to give up trying.

"Are there names and phone numbers on the profiles?"

The three of them looked at each other. "Lacy collected them from us," admitted Babette. "She felt it would be better not to have all that personal information floating around."

No point in beating a dead equine. "Do you remember discussing specific references for Reverend Dark?" I asked.

"You can't call the reverend's current church," said Barney, "because she hasn't told them officially that she's applied for this position. But Reverend Leo was the one who told her about the opening in the first place. Apparently he knew her in school. He'd be a good place to start."

"I'd be happy to follow those leads," I offered. "I'll see if I turn anything up in the church office first." More work for me, but at least I could ask the questions the way I thought they should be asked. Which was probably what Lacy had in mind, I reminded myself. I shouldn't assume she was up to no good. Maybe she just wanted the job done right.

"I loved Reverend Leo," said Babette mournfully. She patted her platinum wig. "When my mother died last year, I was so upset I couldn't even leave my home. He visited several times." She blushed, her fingers plucking at her collar, buttoned tight around her throat. "He always knew what to say. He could make you laugh when you thought the world was ending. He encouraged me to get involved on a church committee this fall after the — attack." Her eyes shone. "You have so much to offer, he said."

I pulled a small notebook out of my purse and scribbled. Observation number one: Babette hadn't moved on to the idea of a new minister — she was stuck in her admiration of the former associate. And she probably wasn't the only parishioner who felt that way. Leo was a charmer. So what?

Observations number two, three, four, and five: Wesley was pressing for Paul. Barney was pressing for Ellen. Babette would drift wherever the wind blew her. Mrs. Wiggett seemed to like Paul well enough, but more than that, she didn't want to agree with Barney or be pushed by Lacy. Or Wesley. She enjoyed a good fight. It was a deadlock. I couldn't imagine how any of this would matter to Meigs.

"Did Lacy seem upset or worried about anything when you saw her last?" I asked.

The door rattled open and Reverend Wesley stumbled in, a blue paper mask covering his mouth and nose, eyes hollow, skin gray, hair dull — he looked like death. And the cough I'd heard at the emergency clinic on Friday night had developed into a wet hack. The whooping cough story — if it was a story — was not at all hard to believe. I swallowed, testing the soreness of my throat. If I hadn't already contracted the bug, I would get another chance.

"Reverend Wesley! What in the world are you doing here? You should be home in bed!" said Mrs. Wiggett. She stood up, crossed the room to draw the minister into our circle, and patted the empty spot on the couch next to me. He sat down and began to cough again. The cough crescendoed from a small tickle to wracking spasms. Red-faced and out of breath, he jerked the mask off, gasping for air.

"You shouldn't be here," said Barney sternly.

Ditto. I inched away along the red velvet couch.

"Sorry," panted Wesley. "I started antibiotics yesterday. Doctor said I'm not contagious. I wouldn't be here if I didn't feel that making a decision was critical."

I glanced at Barney's face — twisted with displeasure. Not about germs, I was willing to guess.

"How are you feeling?" Wesley pointed to the Ace bandage wrapped around my ankle.

"I'm fine," I said with a wave. "Another day and I'll be good as new."

"And Paul?" He looked desperate. "Any news from Paul? He hasn't answered his cell phone. Is he all right? Will he be able to make his interview?"

"Reverend Chanton announced in church that he's expected home later today. As far as we know, everything's on for tomorrow as planned."

"That was a cruel prank," said Mrs. Wiggett. "I hope the police catch that scoundrel soon."

"Prank?" I glanced around the room, watching to see whether any of the others found her "prank" assessment faulty. No one registered a protest.

We chatted for another twenty minutes, plotting the questions we would ask Ellen Dark. Babette would inquire about how she would feel focusing on youth work. Mrs. Wiggett wanted to know how she felt about moving to Guilford. And how about her husband? Did he mind giving up his life in New Hampshire? Barney suggested we stick to her theology of Easter.

"I don't even know what that means," said Babette.

"She'll know," he said, drawing his brows together into a fierce line. "Or else we don't need her."

"How will she feel about working under a man?" Reverend Wesley hacked.

Babette giggled, then clapped a hand to

her mortified face.

"And will she be able to handle a congregation of this size when I'm away?"

"Sounds like we'll have a lively discussion," I said. Hard to imagine she'd want this job by the time we got finished. "Shall we call it an afternoon? I have to pick out a Christmas tree. Wesley, could I speak to you for a moment after?"

He nodded. "I'll be in my office."

Barney pulled me aside as the others filed out of the room. "Just so we're clear," he muttered as they left, "I will not allow him to steamroller us into making a choice. Wesley is supposed to be an adviser, not a . . . a vise grip." His face flushed an unattractive purple.

I nodded and smiled — I don't like someone putting the squeeze on me either. "I'll certainly do my best to make sure everyone has a say."

I picked up my coat and purse and went down the hall to find Wesley. The door to the main office was closed and locked, so I walked a little farther and tapped on his private door.

"Come right in," he said, stepping back and covering his mouth with a hankie to cough. The blue hospital mask still hung around his neck by its strings. "Please sit.

How did the meeting go?"

"Okay," I said, taking a ladder-back chair just in front of his desk. "I'm getting to know them and figuring out where we all stand. I'm going to call a few references and then we'll go ahead with the interviews as they've been scheduled." I pushed my fingers through my hair and massaged the back of my head.

"Sure you don't want to postpone the process until after the holidays? You have a lot on your plate, with Lacy dying, and now the accident with Paul. And you're sick as a dog! Might not hurt to take a little break."

"We've done all the work," he said, his chin jutting forward. "It's just a matter of closing things out." Then he slumped into his chair. "Your cop friend seems to think I killed Lacy."

I felt my shoulders tense. "Why do you say that?"

He frowned and straightened his tie. "He keeps calling and asking for details about what happened Friday night. And he's been asking about Beverly. Beverly, for Gospel's sake."

"What about Beverly?" I asked gently.

"Why she left. Where she is now. Beverly's gone! She's got nothing to do with these problems." He looked tight as a string ready to snap. In therapy, when someone fights that hard to avoid a subject, I'm pretty certain it's worth pursuing. I imagined detective work would feel the same way.

"If there's anything you're not telling him . . . anything at all," I said. "Even if it doesn't seem to have any connection to the case."

He was silent except for the labored breathing.

"Do you have a theory about what happened?" I asked.

Wesley snatched a pencil up from his desktop and began to tap. "Someone doesn't want Paul as our associate pastor. That's all I can come up with."

"But Lacy wasn't in favor of hiring Paul, right?"

He kneaded his forehead and shrugged. "I'm so tired."

"So you're concluding someone doesn't want Paul on board because of his accident?"

"That was no accident," Wesley said, beginning another round of wracking coughs.

"I know." I patted his desk blotter, closest I could come to reassuring him.

"And then this morning the detective asked for a list of the Women's League members attending the supper. The Women's League." He shook his head mournfully. "Sweet, old-fashioned women who call their husbands to kill a spider."

"He has to ask," I said. "They did have a program on poisons this month."

Wesley groaned. "What were they thinking? I should have been paying closer attention."

"You've had a lot on your mind this fall," I said. "As far as you know, was Lacy having family problems? Trouble at work or with a boyfriend?"

Reverend Wesley pursed his lips. "The only trouble I knew about was this damn search committee. I hate to say it, but you might want to watch your back too." He started to cough again and signaled that our conversation was finished. He did look exhausted.

I stood up and pulled my coat on. "You call me if you think of anything. Or need anything. Anything I can do to help."

"You're doing it," he gasped. "Thank you."

I hobbled out to my Honda and fired it up, appreciating the job the sexton had done clearing the pavement. No one — *else* — would slip and fall on his watch. He must be sick about the Crisco incident.

While the engine warmed, I got back out

of the car to scrape a thin coating of ice off the windshield, considering whether I should wait for Meigs to call me. Instead I slid back into the warm car and dialed his number.

"Meigs," he answered.

I turned the radio down. "It's Rebecca. Uh, Dr. Butterman. Rebecca Butterman." Rebecca the imbecile.

"How was the meeting?"

Nothing about my leg or his wife. Fine. I could be all business too.

"One thing stands out loud and plain — these folks are very invested in their choices. Reverend Wesley was there — sick as a dog. He refuses to postpone the process."

"Tell me about your Women's League. Do you have any connection with them?"

"I'm not a member," I said. "It's mostly retired ladies and homemakers because they meet during the day. As I'm sure you saw, I was the speaker at the November luncheon. My topic was giving advice. I asked them to bring in sample problems, but they only came up with two — a disagreement over the place of ivy in a floral arrangement and how to drop someone off your Christmas card list." I laughed, but he didn't join me.

"Any zealots, fanatics, overly religious types in the group?"

"Nothing like that," I insisted. "Listen." I hesitated. "You may have already thought of this, but isn't it possible that Lacy's murder had nothing to do with the church?"

"We've already thought of it," he said brusquely.

Excuse me for living. I took a deep breath. He was probably under a lot of stress. Not that he was going to win Mr. Congeniality otherwise. I'd try to be nice.

"Everything okay?"

"Okay as it can be." He cleared his throat sharply. "As you could see, we had a situation last night."

I waited for him to explain further but he didn't. "How's your wife doing?"

"Up and down," he said.

Blood from a turnip. "I'm sorry," I said. "She seems like a lovely person." I heard a loud voice in the background.

"Hold on," said Meigs.

Voices mumbled, incomprehensible except for the end of one sentence, which sounded like "retching ill."

"Gotta go," Meigs said, back on the phone to me. "Let me know what happens tonight." And he hung up.

I pressed *end* feeling dissatisfied and annoyed. He'd barely seemed interested in my observations. He'd cut me off before I'd

110

even told him about hiding the Crisco. I hadn't mentioned that Lacy might have notes on the candidate references. Or that Wesley was worried about being considered a suspect. Oh hell, let him figure it out. If his wife was ill, he had other priorities. I should cut him some slack.

Text message, I thought suddenly. I pulled my phone back out and struggled with the unfamiliar settings, finally punching in:

Lard/ box in kitch. Call me.

I pushed *send.*

My ankle was stinging like an army of fire ants after the walk from the church to the car. No way I could handle stumping around a farm to choose and then saw down my own tree. I called Janice.

"Let's meet at the Friends of Hammonassett tree sale in Madison," I said when she answered. "I need to take baby steps: I can't face cutting a tree down this year." Better not to tell the truth — that I'd been injured in an absurd accident. She'd worm it out of me soon enough.

"Lord, woman, you need a man!" laughed Janice. "Listen, we're running late. We'll be there as quickly as possible, but I'm guessing forty-five minutes."

CHAPTER 8

I left the church parking lot and headed east, out to Route 1 toward Madison, dreaming of a latte from one of the town's seven coffee shops. With enough caffeine, maybe I could even tackle my Christmas shopping list.

Retching ill. Is that what the other cop said to Meigs? I tried not to picture Alice Meigs violently sick. It was a peculiar turn of phrase. And how would this man even know she wasn't well? Wouldn't she call her husband first? Except he was on his cell phone with me.

As I approached Route 77, I remembered where Lacy Bailes had lived. The cop hadn't said "retching ill," he'd said "Fetching Hill." The search warrant must have come through. I turned north, up Route 77 toward the Fetching Hill condominiums, certain Meigs was headed here too.

With property values and taxes exploding

along the shoreline, Fetching Hill has become very popular with middle-aged and older residents, with its comfortable apartments and distant Long Island Sound view — in the winter. During our brief coffeehour conversation last week, I learned that Lacy moved to this sprawling condo complex several years before. She liked the nofuss home and garden maintenance. Besides, the move cut twenty minutes off her commute to Hartford. Personally, I found it hard enough to handle the politics and personalities in a small condo community.

Plan A: Cruise by her apartment, where I'd stop and tell Meigs the rest of what I knew.

No Plan B.

I turned into the drive and pulled up the hill. It took several winding detours before I found her place, a stone's throw from the tennis courts now thick with snowdrifts. No cop cars here. Also no sign of Detective Meigs's white minivan. What had the other cop said if it wasn't "Fetching Hill"? A psychologist might suggest that I'd heard what I wanted to hear, that I'd conveniently interpreted his gibberish in order to snoop.

Baloney.

Lacy's navy blue Mercedes blocked her driveway, layered with ice and snow. The streets of the complex were clearly zoned no parking. I circled around the block, left my vehicle in the small lot in front of the tennis courts, then limped the half block to Lacy's place. It was still damn cold, the dazzling glare of the sun on snow adding little warmth. Three sets of newspapers — including the *New York Times* Sunday edition by the size of the blue plastic bag — lay in her driveway near the mailbox. I stood by the curb, watching and waiting. A scraping noise echoed nearby. Someone removing the last of yesterday's storm from his sidewalk? But I saw no one.

I swung open the black plastic door on Lacy's mailbox.

"Darned shame about Miss Bailes, isn't it?"

I pressed the door shut and clapped my hand to my chest. "Good God, you scared me half to death."

"Everyone's a little jumpy around here," said a heavy-set man with thick steel gray hair, black galoshes, and no coat — just a faded flannel shirt partly tucked into his blue jeans. His stomach shifted from left to right and back as he lumbered closer, one large hand extended, a snow shovel grasped in the other. "I'm Curt. You one of Lacy's people? Awfully sorry for your loss."

I shook his hand. "No, not exactly." What possible reason would otherwise explain why I was here? *Tell the truth, Rebecca.* "I went to church with her."

"You went to church?"

Probably wondering, as well he might, how that justified snooping through her mail. I certainly wasn't going to start explaining Meigs, the accident, the call Friday night, the Crisco . . .

"The truth is, I'm on a committee with her. I mean she was on the committee and now I'm on it too. She kept all the records herself. It's going to set us back quite a bit if we can't lay our hands on that paper-work." I shrugged. "It was a long shot, but I figured if the cops were still here, they might look around and maybe come up with what I need." I rubbed my hands together briskly, trying to work up a little warmth. "Dumb idea, huh?"

"My father used to say you're only dumb if you don't give it your all. Took me fifty years to figure out what the hell he meant." Curt cackled. "The cops haven't been here since they showed up late Friday. Woke up Sharon — that's my wife. I never sleep much anyway. I'm on workers' compensation — forklift got the best of me and my back hasn't been the same since."

116

He reached around with one big, gloved hand and patted the small of his back.

"Anyway, some of the local yokels came back around yesterday morning. They wouldn't tell me anything about what happened, can you imagine? She was our closest neighbor! I think they were pissed because I'm not much of a witness." He laughed like a goof. "But what kind of yahoo would be skulking around the neighbor's house in weather this damn cold? Besides, I grew up in the sixties and we don't tell the fuzz more than absolutely necessary. Hey, maybe I'm a suspect, not a witness." His eyes glittered like black buttons as he laughed again, then stopped abruptly. "Did you know her well?"

"Not really." I was beginning to see a glimmer of possibility. He might not talk to the cops, but maybe he'd help me understand what had happened to Lacy. "Gosh, it's so sad, isn't it?"

"Sad it is. She seemed a little lonely to us. My wife, Sharon, carried over a sweet potato pie the week Lacy moved in," he explained. "And offered to water her plants and bring in the mail and feed the cat if she went out of town.

"She's friendly, my wife." The big man grinned. "Lacy didn't have a cat, but if she ever got one, my wife was in line to take care of it." He laughed heartily. "I don't believe she was used to neighbors being quite so neighborly, but we feel it's the right thing to do. So we gave her our key and then she told us where she kept her spare. Just for emergencies only," he added, nodding his head and winking.

He jangled the giant key ring clipped to his belt buckle and waited for me to say something. I could imagine him hulking over Lacy Bailes until she had no choice but to tender her key secrets.

"I'm sure she appreciated your kindness." I turned and started back to my car. "Nice to meet you. Hope that back feels better." I paused and faced him again. "Say, listen, did you notice whether Lacy had any visitors on Friday?"

"Sure, she did." He grinned.

This guy was a nut. "Male or female?"

"Hard to say. It was dark and they were all bundled up, but I'd vote at least one of each."

"Would you recognize their cars?"

"Most people park down the street where you are," he said. "So I can't really match 'em up with their rides."

"Did you by any chance tell the police?"

"They didn't ask," he said, knocking his

skull with his fist. "Dumb as rocks."

"Thanks again." I nodded and limped down the sidewalk.

"Now why did you say you were here?" His voice floated after me.

I turned around a second time. "She was heading up the committee that's choosing a new minister for the Shoreline Congregational Church in Guilford. Now we're in a bind because we don't have her notes or her folders or anything."

"I could show you around," he offered.

The idea made me queasy.

"She gave us permission," he said, beckoning me forward.

I hesitated, biting my lower lip. Why was he willing to do this? Nosiness, boredom, one-upping the cops? Maybe all three. Meigs would be furious. But this wasn't breaking and entering, just a walk-through with an overly friendly neighbor — a neighbor with a key and permission to use it. I couldn't justify it any better than I could snooping in Lacy's mail. But I wanted to know what had happened. Most of all, I wanted the search committee over and done. If her notes were lying out in plain sight —

"Come on," Curt said, starting to the back of the condo.

"Maybe if we could just look for those papers," I said, tripping down the pathway after him, our shoulders dipping into matching limps.

"Don't worry, we won't touch anything. You never know when Smokey might make another visit."

For a big man with an apparent disability, Curt moved quickly as he darted to the cellar door under the porch. He felt along the inside of the main porch beam, stopping to extract a key hanging from a nail. He glanced back at me, his smile shadowed by the deck overhead, and unlocked the door with a practiced twist. He'd done this before.

He pointed to my boots.

"Shoes off," he said, prying his own feet out of his enormous galoshes. "Lacy was a stickler about her carpet."

And neither one of us wanted our footprints on the authorities' radar. My stomach churned, as I suddenly recognized how badly I wanted to show off, show Meigs how good my powers of observation were. This was a harebrained stunt and I knew it. Meigs would be apoplectic if he found out.

By the time we'd climbed the cellar stairs, my breath was coming fast and shallow. I'd been in a dead woman's house earlier this fall, and it hadn't turned out well. I sucked in a lungful of cold, stale air and tugged my coat tighter around my waist.

Curt's booming voice cut through my nervous thoughts. "Feels like they turned the heat way down. Didn't take 'em long to get her out — maybe fifteen minutes after the ambulance came. They hadn't pulled the sheet over her head or anything, but from the way they were moving, I had a feeling it wasn't going to be a happy ending."

Just what I needed, a treatise on Lacy's last hours. Why in the name of God had I agreed to come in?

"Some kind of poison, that's my guess," he went on without any encouragement, looking at me for confirmation.

I kept my face blank and my mouth shut.

"She had a cleaning lady come once a week," said Curt. "Can you imagine? How messy could one lady be? It's not like she had kids or a dog or what have you traipsing through. Like Sharon has me for example." He chortled. He was breathing hard too, though more likely from the bulk he carried than anxiety.

"Here's the living room. You see what I mean? What's to do in this place, run a duster over the knickknacks, that's all there is."

Lacy had collected Hummel figurines — angels with musical instruments and children bearing apples, fishing poles, and baking supplies, all displayed on the Victorian end tables and bookcase. Hand-painted and high-priced or not, I just didn't get it. An empty wastebasket stood next to the end table. A half glass of water had wept a white ring onto the polished dark wood. A purple mohair throw was bunched on the arm of the couch. Had to have been here that Wesley found her.

"Kitchen's this way," Curt explained.

I padded down the hall behind him, my teeth chattering lightly.

Curt turned and grinned. "It's the mirror image of our place, that's how I know it all so well. She would eat breakfast here" — he pointed to a glossy pine table striped with a lace runner — "or sometimes on the deck in the summer. But otherwise, she was at work. We hardly saw her. My Sharon asked her over for supper a couple of times but she always said no."

The kitchen was perfectly orderly, not a fork out of place. The only personal touch was a handwritten note stuck to the refrigerator with a faux-Hummel magnet:

Polish the silver today if you have the

time. LB.

I was tempted to open cupboards and fridge — see what kind of cook she was: Food does make the woman. But that wasn't my business. I noticed the row of red lights holding steady across the top of her dishwasher, indicating the wash cycle was complete. Even on the night she died, Lacy Bailes was neat.

"Did she have an office?" I asked.

"Second floor," said Curt, "this way."

We marched up the stairs and Curt turned right.

"This is her bedroom," I said, stopping in the doorway.

"The front room is larger," Curt told me, "but you don't hear the traffic noise in back. Not that there's any traffic to speak of, but some people just have a hard time sleeping."

Blue-flowered curtains matched the quilt on Lacy's double bed. Crocheted toppers protected the mahogany surfaces of the dresser and nightstands. I glanced over the paperbacks stacked in her bookcase — mostly romances. Not what I would have predicted given her crusty exterior, but then I didn't know her that well.

"Come on and take a look around," Curt

said, waving me forward.

I stared back. Who died and made him king? "I'd just like to see the office. If her notes aren't right out on the desk, I'm out of luck."

He shrugged. "Whatever." He pushed past me and we walked down the hall. The office was just as neat as the rest of the house, no stacks of papers on the file cabinet, no randomly scribbled notes on her desk, no photos, no scratch pads. One brochure poked out from under the telephone. It had a picture of a man slumped on a table, a liquor bottle in his hand. The title was "The Merry-Go-Round of Denial."

Curt pulled a Swiss Army knife out of his pants pocket. "If the drawers are locked, I can show you whatever you need."

I'd had enough. Then we heard the sound of an engine rumbling. Curt hurried over to the window, peered out, and then ducked back against the wall.

"Son of a bastard," he said. "What the hell? It's the fuzz. We have to move!"

My heart pounded as we raced back down two flights of stairs, slipped into our shoes, and waited. What would I possibly say to the police about why I'd been caught in a dead woman's basement forty-eight hours after she'd been murdered? One thing for sure: I wasn't leaving it up to Curt.

After a minute, my eyes grew used to the darkness. I tried to stay calm by cataloging the contents of Lacy's basement: a water heater, a treadmill covered in clear plastic, two rakes, a shovel, shelves loaded with bags of bulbs, bonemeal, fertilizer . . . It felt like hours, but my watch said we'd only waited a few minutes when Curt announced he'd heard the cruiser pull away.

"Whee-ha," he yelped. "That was a close call, eh? Must have been a routine drive-by. Good damn thing you parked down the road."

I just stared. "Let's get the hell out." When we were safely back on the sidewalk, blinking in the sun, I said good-bye and took off for my car. Now I'd have to figure out how to send Meigs up to talk with Curt without giving myself away.

I drove to the tree sale at Hammonassett State Park, my body heavy with relief, my mind still whirling with the aftershocks of stupidity. I snapped an imaginary rubber band.

I spotted Janice and Brittany before I'd even gotten out of the car. They looked adorable, dressed in matching red coats with fleece-lined hoods and plaid trim. I felt a wash of love and, just as quickly, amazement. How does my sister manage to live a life like a Martha Stewart magazine when mine resembles a tabloid shocker, only not nearly that thrilling?

We exchanged hugs and started down the first aisle of trees, Brittany skipping ahead. Janice balanced a succession of trees on their trunks so I could study their size and shape. I circled to the back of the one she held, full in front but with major branches reaching clear down to the bottom of the stump; it would be hell to stand. I flicked my fingers and she let it drop.

"Where were you yesterday?" she asked, a mixture of concern and suspicion in her voice. "And what's wrong with your leg?"

I told her about the church supper, soft-pedaling my tumble, sweetening the pot with Bob. "He seems nice," I said. "He went to Princeton, he has money, he's tall and nice-looking."

The tree she was holding flopped to the frozen ground in a cloud of needles. She broke into a smile. "Why don't you bring him to Christmas dinner?"

"Janice, he hasn't even called me yet. It would be a great understatement to say we're not at the family holiday introductions stage."

"You're so old-fashioned," she said. "Today's men need a little push. I've told you about Jimmy and me, the first time I met him?"

Of course she'd told me. They'd been married close to ten years.

"I found your tree, Aunt Rebecca," Brittany yelled. "Come look. Then can we go get some hot chocolate? I'm freeeezing!"

We tromped over to the next row. I met my sister's eyes over the top of Brittany's choice: It was short, lopsided, almost cylindrical.

My sister laughed. "At school, they'd call that a tree with 'special needs.' "

"Who else is going to pick this one if you don't?" said Brittany. "This one needs you."

We loaded the tree into the back of Janice's Expedition and returned to my condo in Guilford. Bernd Becker, our complex handyman, was spreading salt on the walk in front of the clubhouse. He and our church sexton could rule the world if they decided they were interested.

"Let me give you ladies a hand with that," he said.

"Is he married?" Janice whispered.

I slapped her hand and placed my finger to my lips. "Stop that."

After Bernd had wrestled the tree into its

stand, I helped Brittany dump a block of Swiss chocolate into a pan of milk. "Keep stirring until it's melted. Otherwise it will burn."

I popped a collection of carols into the CD player and collapsed on the couch next to Janice.

"I love Christmas." She draped an arm around my shoulders. "Don't you?"

"Not so much," I said in a low voice.

The idea that had been nagging me over the past few weeks pushed to the surface. Should I raise it? With Janice, there's never a great time to rock the boat. I rolled my neck to the left and then to the right, hearing the tension crackle. In fact, I had mentioned this to her last September. Her method of dealing with it was to pretend she hadn't heard.

I sighed. "I know I brought this up a couple of months ago, and you weren't a big fan. But I feel like I need to make some peace with our father. I'm going to try tracking him down."

She drew herself up stiffly, making a space between us. I patted her knee. "You don't have to be part of it if you don't want to, but it's something I have to do."

She frowned. "Why?"

"I don't think I'll be able to make a

relationship work without putting that piece in place."

"That's ridiculous," Janice said. "Mine works just fine."

Think before you speak, I told myself, feeling the mounting irritation. "Maybe we don't want the same thing."

"You're saying there's something wrong with my marriage?" She stood, hands on hips, lips pursed, pulsing with outrage.

She was right — I don't want her marriage. Jim works ungodly hours and travels at least twice a month for days at a time. They see each other on Saturdays, if he isn't playing hockey or poker in the winter and golf in the summer, and probably bump into each other in the night. Knowing Janice, she schedules sex once a week. Or twice, if that's what her women's magazines say will keep her man from straying.

I'd waited too long to answer.

She grabbed their coats from the rocking chair, dislodging Spencer. "I truly don't understand why you'd want to hunt down a man who's been missing" — she practically spit — "our whole lives." Tears pushed into her eyes. "And it won't just affect you, Rebecca. If you drag that bastard into your life, he screws mine up too. Brittany, we're leaving," she called.

"But I didn't get my chocolate! Mom, it's almost melted."

"Now!"

Janice whirled out of the door, my niece in tow. Just as quickly, she was back, a flimsy cardboard box in her hands. She thrust it at me. "Merry Christmas. It's fragile."

Like you, I thought. The door slammed behind her. What on earth made me think this discussion would turn out any differently? At some point we'd have to talk about why she'd overreacted, without me using that label, of course.

I deposited the box under the crooked tree, then sniffed. Something was burning. I hurried out to the kitchen and yanked Brittany's hot chocolate off the stove, now thickened and scorched. I dropped the pan into the sink, filled it with water, and glanced at the wall clock. My Currier and Ives moment with my family had lasted less than forty-five minutes.

Somehow, I'd smooth things over with Janice and then start in again later: after Christmas, more slowly. I hit *play* on the answering machine, sick of problems.

"Rebecca, it's Bob. I had such a nice time with you last night. Any chance you're free for an impromptu dinner?"

The idea made me tired.

Next came Jillian, my editor for the "Late Bloomer" column at *Bloom!*

"I know it's a Sunday," she chirped, "but no rest for the advice givers! How are you coming on the Christmas column? Can you get it to me by tomorrow? Give me a buzz."

I groaned, opened the computer file containing Christmas-themed complaints from readers, and pulled up the first one. Anything would do.

Dear Dr. Aster:

Christmas is on the horizon and with it, my annual lament: My husband has no taste when it comes to gifts. As many hints as I offer (and believe me, they aren't subtle), he gives me something unusable. Last year it was an entire set of lumpy hand-thrown pottery dishes — not even dishwasher safe. Has he not heard of lead glazes? I've already snooped in his shopping bags — it appears I have a nightgown only his grandmother would wear in my future. Can you help?

Disappointed in Darien

Dear Disappointed:
Let's revisit the original meaning of

Christmas. As legend tells it, the only gift in those early days was a special baby. No lingerie, no unattractive tableware, no whining wives . . .

Forget it. I had a naked Christmas tree with "special needs" and no ornaments, my sister wasn't speaking to me, I'd trespassed in a dead woman's home, and based on the rasping feeling in my throat, I had a fledgling case of whooping cough. I'd try again tomorrow.

I was flat out of both tact and good advice tonight.

CHAPTER 9

After washing my face, slathering on extra moisturizer, and popping more Advil, I drove back over to the church for the session with Ellen Dark. An attitude adjustment was in order: The very last thing I wanted to do at this moment was attend another meeting. I perked up a little at seeing lights on in the church office. With any luck, I'd catch the secretary and pump her for the latest on Paul's condition — and Lacy's murder. And see if she could save me some time by putting her hands on the missing committee minutes.

Instead of chatty Nancy, I found Mrs. McCabe pulling a clear plastic cover over the computer keyboard. She had removed last night's antlers, but bejeweled Christmas trees dangled from her earlobes. I tapped on the glass door and she leaped up from the secretary's chair, clutching her chest. I hurried into the office. "I'm so sorry, I didn't mean to scare you!"

Patting her bosom, she said: "Everyone's a little jumpy around here." She frowned and pointed to my foot. "That was quite a tumble you took last night How's your ankle?"

"A little swollen," I said, rolling my shoulders. In fact every body part felt bruised and sore this evening, but she wouldn't want to hear all that. "It'll be fine by tomorrow. Thanks for asking. Is Nancy around?"

"She had to rush home to Maryland," said Mrs. McCabe. "Her mother's having surgery, and they're not at all sure she'll survive it. Nancy's been back and forth all month, but maybe this will be the end of it. Lord willing," she tacked on.

I groaned. "What a Christmas."

"Anything I can help you with?"

"Have we heard from Paul?"

"Poor Paul," she said, taking her seat again, head bobbing. "He's home. He called in for his messages so I talked to him myself." She explained that the doctor had prescribed bed rest but that Paul had just laughed — it was Christmas, the busiest religious holiday of the year, and it wouldn't do to have all the ministers out of commission.

"So I told him, absolutely do not come in

tomorrow before your interview with the committee." She wagged her finger for emphasis. "Men don't know how to take care of themselves, do they?" She pointed to the slash of light leaking from under Reverend Wesley's door. "Especially ministers."

I stroked my chin and grunted. In my experience, men know these things well enough but prefer to act helpless. Reverend Wesley is a good example. Since Beverly left him earlier in the fall, Mrs. McCabe and Nancy Wilcox have been fighting to watch over him. No funny business, of course, just old-fashioned caretaking.

"You were at the supper last night," I said. "Did you notice anyone in the kitchen or the hall who shouldn't have been there?"

"The Crisco," said Mrs. McCabe, nodding. She picked up the corner of her sweater and polished fingerprints off the edge of the desk. "The police asked the same thing. It was such a madhouse. And we do get outsiders coming to dinner . . ." She raised her eyebrows — was she curious about Bob or Meigs or both? "I wish I could help."

"How about when you first got to the staircase — anyone there you didn't recognize?"

"Not that I can think of. I was so worried about you two . . ." She straightened the carved wooden figurines in the manger scene on the desk, then got to her feet. "Off I go. The sexton will be looking for supper."

"One more thing," I said. "Lacy Bailes was making calls and taking notes for the committee but no one seems to know where they are. Any ideas about that?"

"I can try." She tapped briskly across the room to a file cabinet against the wall and slid open the second drawer. "Here's all your search committee info." She pulled out a fat green binder and riffled through the pages. "Suggestions on constructing your church profile, choosing an interim minister, communicating with the congregation . . ."

I held my hand up. Too late to reinvent that wheel. Then she extracted another small sheaf of papers and fanned through them quickly. "Here's the data from the membership survey: what our people think are the most important qualities in a minister and what issues need to be addressed first."

"I will take a look at those," I said, crossing the room to take them from her and tucking them into my purse. I was curious about what our church members had requested and whether this committee had paid any attention.

"I don't see anything from Lacy. I'll look more thoroughly tomorrow. Her notes could have been misfiled or who knows what."

"Great. Thanks."

She gathered her coat and purse, shut off the copier and the lights, and followed me into the hall. She locked the door behind us. "Good luck with Mrs. Dark. She seems like a nice person, but she's awfully chatty, isn't she? I may be old-fashioned, but I've never taken to women in this job. Men are the real leaders. We just aren't built the same way."

She wasn't old-fashioned: She was lumbering through the Dark Ages. But I didn't have the energy or the time to lecture her about feminism and the importance of women supporting women. "We won't hire anyone who can't do the job well," I said briskly. "Good night."

I limped down the hall to the parlor. None of the other committee members had arrived. *First come, first served,* I thought, choosing a comfortable wing chair. I flipped through the surveys while waiting for the rest of the committee. The people seemed to want an inspirational speaker; someone great with kids, good with the sick folks and those recently bereaved; a good leader;

comfortable with asking for money; concerned with relationships to other community churches and the world at large . . . even a saint couldn't live up to this.

I rested my head against the back of the chair and closed my eyes. In spite of her Neanderthal politics, Mrs. McCabe seemed to have a pretty good handle on managing the ins and outs of the church office. It would probably be fine with her if Nancy didn't come back at all. I chuckled, wondering how well Mrs. McCabe managed "the sexton." It does annoy me when women refer to their husbands by their function, though Mark might have enjoyed being called "the doctor."

My throat felt worse by the minute. It had been a rotten day and I wanted to be home in bed, wrapped in flannel, sipping tea, my cat on my lap, my ankle on ice.

The other members of the search committee, plus Reverend Wesley, trickled in and by five past five we'd gotten settled. Then Ellen Dark appeared, filling the doorway and crackling with energy. With her barrel shape and red and white dress, she looked like an oversized can of Campbell's soup. Chicken noodle maybe or minestrone. I could tell I was getting hungry. She plunked down on the uncomfortable couch next to the hacking Reverend Wesley. "Sounds like you should be home in bed, young man," she said, patting his arm.

"I'm on the upswing," he said, unconvincingly.

"Thanks for coming," Barney Brooks told her. "We're glad you've had the chance to spend some time in the community this weekend."

"I simply adore this shoreline area," she said. "The homes and decorations are so classic and the people so friendly. I was warned that the stiff Yankee reserve was even worse in Connecticut than New Hampshire, but I haven't seen that." She broke into a radiant smile.

A backhanded compliment if I'd ever heard one. Who the hell described us as stiff Yankees? I reminded myself to back off and stand by to counsel and nudge as needed.

One by one, the committee asked the questions that we'd rehearsed earlier. Ellie, as she insisted we call her, told Babette that she loved children of all ages and was very enthusiastic about tackling the youth program. She'd heard that our attendance had dropped quite noticeably over the past year and she had some excellent thoughts on how to improve that.

Barney professed to being satisfied with her theological explanations, though they were unintelligible to me. The questions seemed designed more to show off his knowledge than help us decide on the right candidate.

Finally, Ellie assured Reverend Wesley that she was absolutely looking forward to working as a team. "Adam and Eve, Jesus and Mary, Wesley and Ellie," she said with a chuckle. "There's plenty of precedent in the Bible for a good male/female team."

I smiled politely. *Sweet* Jesus. And Mary, and Adam and Eve. She was including herself in some pretty exalted company.

Although there was nothing major to find fault with, I wasn't warming up to Ellie. I might have a hard time liking anyone, feeling this achy and weak. Or maybe it was the vibration of underlying certainty that she had a lock on the position. The bizarre thought came to mind that *she* had killed Lacy. For what, supporting another candidate? Absurd. Besides, wasn't Lacy her second-biggest fan? I laid a hand on my forehead, testing for fever.

I blew out a grateful sigh when Ellie finally left the room. My head was spinning but I forced myself to remember why I was there. Among other things, Detective Meigs had asked me to feel out what Lacy thought of the candidates without asking directly.

"How did Lacy like Ellen?" I asked, too tired and annoyed to be subtle.

"She liked her very much," said Barney. "Being a strong woman herself, she appreciated chutzpah, guts, and spirit in a candidate."

"They never even met," Mrs. Wiggett protested.

"They met at a conference last fall and she'd spoken to her on the phone several times," Barney insisted.

This was going nowhere. "The church office doesn't seem to have your meeting minutes or any notes indicating that Lacy called the candidates' references," I said.

"Typical!" snapped Barney. "Why did she have to be so goddamn secretive and controlling?"

Babette's eyes widened and I cut right in.

"I'll be happy to follow up tomorrow. I'll try to have something by the time we meet with Paul. Did we say seven? I feel a little flu-ish and I'm headed home to bed. Good night all."

I dragged home, snapped the dead bolts, and scooped up Spencer, comforted by his rhythmic purr. He perched on the counter, watching as I moved a tub of chicken rice soup from the freezer to the microwave. Once every two months or so, I cook up and freeze a batch of chicken soup for just this kind of emergency. It's made from scratch, from my grandmother's recipe: homemade stock, extra celery, and don't drain off the flavor by skimming all the fat. Sometimes I add a splash of Japanese soy sauce or a pinch of cilantro. My mouth watered. This way, I'm not so tempted to feel sorry for myself when I'm sick or out of sorts. I poured a tall glass of ginger ale on ice and sank into the couch, letting the worries of the long day wash over me.

How had I gone from a relatively normal person on Friday to a regular at the emergency clinic by Sunday, embroiled in search committee politics and lurking around a dead woman's home? For the first time, I allowed myself to review what I'd seen there. Lacy was a fiend for organization and neatness. I couldn't even remember spotting the requisite messy pile of unpaid bills. On a side note, unlikely that she wouldn't have (A) followed up on the references or (B) kept careful notes. And I hadn't seen clues about why anyone would want to kill her. What, the cleaning woman didn't want to polish the silver? Lacy had stolen a prized

Hummel figurine from a competitor in a vicious auction?

I wished I hadn't been so rattled by the close call with the cops — maybe I would have pressed Curt for more useful details about Lacy's Friday night visitors. In fact, he'd been rather coy about the subject. How would I break that bit of news to Meigs? Was there a way to point him to the neighbor without implicating my own foolishness? I didn't see how. He might be less angry if I could provide real data, like who, where, what, and when.

I put off calling Meigs until I'd finished the chicken rice soup and half a sleeve of Saltine crackers. Then I washed the dishes, swept the kitchen floor, wiped the counters down with Windex, and got into my nightgown and slippers. I still felt awkward about bothering him, considering his minimal interest in me or the case last night. Maybe I should let him call me. But he specifically told me to phone him after the interview with Reverend Dark. He said he'd be working the night shift.

With no other obvious ideas for procrastination, I dialed his cell, which funneled me to voicemail after one ring. Had he forgotten to recharge his phone? Maybe he was that kind of man: Good with the details of his work — I'd seen that with my case last fall — but not with personal stuff. Not that this call was personal.

So I tried the station too. He was not in and the dispatcher had no idea when to expect him.

"Could you tell him Dr. Butterman called?" Hard not to be annoyed.

I got into bed with my laptop and a cup of tea. My throat felt like hell — burned and swollen. I typed "whooping cough symptoms" into the Google search bar and clicked on a British doctor's site. He reported that the disease is caused by bacteria and spread through close contact; the bacteria are propelled through the air by coughing. Further down on his homepage, he'd posted links to sound tracks of both children and adults with the cough. I clicked on the adult male segment and listened to twenty disgusting seconds of a man with a choking cough that ended in suffocating paroxysms. Sounded just like Reverend Wesley in the parlor.

And then I remembered where I'd heard it even earlier — waiting in line to shake Wesley's hand after a service two weeks ago. Lacy Bailes had coughed with the same intensity.

CHAPTER 10

I woke up with a runny nose, throbbing sinuses, and a stuffy head. Swallowing experimentally — throat still sore — I began to cough. Then I pulled up the whooping cough website and listened to the repulsive track again — my sound bite was not the same.

"You have a good old-fashioned, miserable cold, that's all," I told myself.

I brewed coffee, fed Spencer, and nibbled at a piece of toast while considering whether I should go to work. Some patients might object to me spreading germs in their breathing space, but in the end, I decided it would cause more trouble to stay home. In the process of calling to reschedule each of my five patients, I'd have to deal with their disappointment, concern, and, in some cases, panic. Easier just to pop Sudafed and aspirin, avoid shaking hands, and ford through the day.

Backing out of the garage, I spotted a blur of yellowed fur against the snowbank: Babette's little white dog, Wilson, trailing his leash behind him. I slammed on the brakes in time to avoid hitting him and rolled my window down to apologize. Babette whisked the dog into her arms.

"Wilson!" she scolded. "You have to watch where you're going. This is what happens when you run away from Mommy."

"So sorry," I said, honking into a Kleenex.

"Are you going to be able to make it tonight?" asked Babette. "You sound awful."

"I'll make it," I said. "If it kills me." Babette startled. "Sorry," I said again.

"I get so nervous in those meetings," said Babette. "I didn't realize how hard it would be when they asked. But I guess it's important to finish what we begin." She squared her shoulders. "Ms. Dark seems like the right one for the job. Doesn't she?" Her forehead creased with worried lines.

"I think she thinks she's right for the job," I said, also thinking it must be agonizing to be inside Babette's head: chugging forward, backpedaling madly, never certain.

"Funny thing is," Babette continued, "I didn't get the idea that Lacy was all that hot on her."

I kept very still. She didn't very often have the nerve to speak for herself.

She rubbed her cheek against Wilson's topknot. "But I know she wasn't in favor of Paul. She felt we needed a woman. I'm not really a women's libber — if a man is best for the job, then let him have it. But if Reverend Leo likes her, I guess that's good enough for me." She tugged on the mohair scarf wrapped around her platinum beehive. "I didn't want to say this in the group," she whispered, "but how did Lacy talk them into letting her keep all the notes herself? And letting her call all the references? Not that there's anything wrong with that," she added hastily. "Have a good day and see you tonight. Say bye-bye to the doctor, Wilson." She worked the dog's front paw into a grudging wave and headed back toward her condo.

Winding through Guilford, I puzzled over Babette's nervous yakking. Did she mean that Lacy wanted a woman, any woman, at any cost? And why had she kept a death grip on the committee? I pulled onto the highway and concentrated on navigating the stop-and-go Monday morning rush hour to New Haven without a fender bender.

After meeting with my first three patients, I

felt even worse than when I'd started, sick and glum. And it wasn't just the head cold. The holidays bring a special kind of lament to therapy — parents who split on Christmas Eve, presents of clothes instead of toys or a puppy, families who will never travel over the river and through the woods because Grandmother is psycho. I have to remind myself that while the specific content might change, the work doesn't. People who feel deprived at the holidays often feel the same way the rest of the year. I help them explore the historical meaning, look for ripples into the present, and work on lifting some of the old weight up and leaving it behind. With patience, the results can feel like the optical illusion that changes from an old hag to a young woman.

Speaking of weight, last night's message from Jillian about the special Christmas advice column hung over me like a five hundred pound marlin on a gaff hook. The juices were not flowing this morning — only mucus. Although giving advice is definitely easier than therapy. Unless I think too much about the responsibility of half a million women waiting to hear me tell them whether they should leave the bum, even though it's Christmas Eve.

I remembered my favorite advice diva's

admonition: When in doubt, write about cheating. Your audience will always relate: They've done it and are wracked with guilt, they're considering it and are desperate for encouragement, they've had it done to them and want to see the bastard punished, or they just plain want to enjoy the vicarious thrill. Or the diva's scolding. I opened the advice column file on my laptop, sorted through the folder of readers' problems, and started in.

Dear Dr. Aster:
Two months ago, I threw my husband out when I finally realized he'd been sleeping with one of his coworkers for the past year. It seemed so clearly the right thing to do at the time. But now I'm beginning to realize the cost of my dramatic scene. First of all, the kids are a wreck, bugging me constantly about when Daddy's coming home. Even little things are bringing me down — he always set up the lighted reindeer on the roof, for example. No way I'm making that climb. And how the heck do I handle Christmas, which we've always shared with his family? Did I make a mistake by throw-

ing him out?

Sincerely,
Waffling in Walla Walla

With this kind of problem, it's hard to improve on the question Ann Landers used to pose to unhappy wives: Are you better off with him or without him? But I had to try.

Dear Waffling:

Oh, how Dr. Aster wishes she had a simple answer. But there's nothing simple about one's first lonely Christmas, is there? Especially when TV, radio, and shopwindows tell you every other girl is getting dancing sugarplums. Allow me to pose a few questions.

What kind of contact have you had with your husband since the big "scene"? If you've already heard from his lawyer about property and custody, chances are he's ready to move on even if you aren't — regardless of whether it's Christmas, New Year's, or National Marital Reconciliation Day.

Second, the infidelity aside, how was the relationship going? In other

words, did your husband hoist the flag of surrender after years of rough seas or could this possibly have been a short-lived, though humiliating and despicable lapse? Whichever way the wind blows, you'll have lots to sort out, both with him and without him. Ending a marriage — even one not made in heaven — is a major loss. As with a death, you'll need time and patience to rebound. Don't hesitate to ask for help — the professional kind. Even if you don't end up living happily ever after with your husband, do try healing the rift enough to be civil. Your children will be thankful, and your future relationships will benefit too.

Most important, please don't rush to make a decision. You may have to suffer through the pain of a lonely holiday to reach the joyous New Year on the other side.

Good luck and be careful!

Not much danger *that* column would titillate readers. I pulled a rubber band out of my desk drawer and snapped it onto my wrist. I would not revisit the trauma with my own husband.

Instead, I puzzled over why Meigs would have interrogated Wesley about Beverly and their broken marriage. And wondered again why the relationship had fallen apart. Reverend Wesley embroiled in a hot and heavy affair simply didn't ring true. His wife — now that was a different matter. She had always struck me as the kind of woman who was dressed for something better than any place she was actually expected to be. At least in our little town. A whiff of expensive perfume, pearls that didn't look like imitation, stylish clothes that could not be found at Talbot's or, God help us, Wal-Mart; we just don't see that sort of thing at the Shoreline Congregational Church Women's League events.

Looking back to our single "counseling" session, I remembered Wesley insisting that the church wouldn't really miss Beverly's presence. After all, she'd skipped more and more of these functions as they'd gotten closer to separating, especially the evening events. I imagined her holed up in the bedroom of their parsonage — located across the street from the church — shades drawn tight and phone ringer off, fed up with the bottomless pit of needy parishioners.

I tried to picture how hard it might be to

tell your husband — *the minister* — that you wanted out. I could imagine Beverly Sandifer snapping, broken like a twig by the heavy mantle of her husband's profession, and then taking that wild step — an affair — that would end up severing the tie. But who in his right mind would get involved with the minister's wife? And was any of this related to Lacy?

Matching whooping cough symptoms or not, it was damn hard to imagine Lacy and Wesley together. As a recovered alcoholic, she liked her life tidy: That much was clear. And having a fling with the minister would be anything but neat.

I tried Meigs one more time, past annoyed and now a little worried that he hadn't called. This time I left a voicemail on his cell phone.

"Rebecca Butterman here. Hope you got the message that I called last night. I don't have anything too big to report so far. We met with Ellen Dark. She seems awfully confident about her chances, like maybe someone told her she was a shoo-in. Even though Babette says Lacy wasn't that crazy about her, so who would have told her that? Anyway, did you get my text about the can in the kitchen? It's under the coffee cups —"

My cell phone ran out of bars before I could confess the visit to Lacy's home. If he didn't care enough about the case to call me back, then he couldn't expect to glean every detail. Besides, the more I thought about it, the more it made sense just to swing back up to Fetching Hill, knock on Curt's door, and insist that he tell the cops the facts. Then I wouldn't have to be involved at all. But definitely not today.

I washed my hands, brushed my hair, and patted lotion on the reddened skin around my nostrils. Nothing less glamorous than a damn cold. I walked the three blocks to my therapist's office, figuring the snowdrifts would make parking on Trumbull Street even more daunting than usual. Besides, the sun was out and the temperature was warming slightly.

"I have a cold," I told Dr. Goldman as soon as I sat down. "And it's been a horrible couple of days." It came out *howwable.*

I described the trouble at the church and how I'd allowed myself to get pulled in. Then I held my hand up. "Before you start making interpretations about my tendency to take on problems that aren't mine, there's something more important."

He nodded gravely, then passed me a box of Kleenex when I started to sniffle. "Janice and I had a fight. Over my father."

"Your father?" He tented his fingers, his hooded eyes brightening. Nothing perks a therapist up more quickly than a big development on an ancient subject.

"Not my father exactly. Just that I've decided I want to look for him and Janice is against it. He could be dead for all I know. He could be a major jerk. That's not really in question, is it, given that he left two little girls who'd already lost their mother?"

"You've been angry at him for a long time," said Dr. Goldman. "And now you're scared about what you really might find."

I waved him off. "Anyway, I'm going to start looking. Once we get through Christmas." We sat in silence for several minutes.

"What are you thinking?" he asked.

"It's that cop," I said. "Jack Meigs. I met him when my neighbor was killed?" I glanced over to see if he remembered.

He nodded, his eyes narrowed, watching. I'd been dancing around the subject for months and Goldman was no dunce.

"His wife has ALS. He was going to ask for a separation and then he found out she was sick." I blew my nose and dabbed at my eyes. "I fell down some stairs Saturday night and got taken to the clinic. Meigs was there with his wife, Alice. She had some

155

trouble breathing."

I found myself sniffling all over again, gasping a little for air. "I'm not upset about him per se. I don't really know him."

"If it's not him, can you put your finger on what's making you sad?" Dr. Goldman asked.

"Something about him being a cop. To protect and to serve and all that. He was very sweet with his wife." I sighed heavily and tried to smile through my chapped lips. "Time to move on and date a real guy who's available. Bob, for example." I slapped my forehead. "Damn! I never called him back. Angie's going to wring my neck."

Dr. Goldman shifted forward in his leather chair. "You started out today talking about your father. Does the detective remind you of him?"

"How can anyone remind me of him?" I snapped. "I was a kid when he left."

Silence.

"You think these feelings about Meigs are related to tracking my father down."

"Maybe." He shrugged.

I groaned. "I hate the holidays. They're brutal if you don't have the right kind of family." I closed my eyes and popped the rubber band on the inside of my wrist, hoping he wouldn't notice; he wasn't a big fan of behavior modification techniques. "At least I'm not dead, like Lacy."

He raised his eyebrows to delicate points. I was an expert at reading the meaning by now: He knew I was avoiding the issue but he was giving me rope.

"It seems odd, doesn't it, that someone would be murdered over a search committee? Assuming, of course, that it was murder rather than a heart attack. Either Lacy pissed someone off in a big way or she was keeping someone's secret. No one on the committee is really talking about either of those possibilities, except poor, hapless Babette. And she doesn't have the nerve to say it aloud." I tried to blow my nose but everything had swollen tight with the crying. "I suppose over the next few days the picture will get more clear. The detective wants me to gather the data and report it to him and then let him move the pieces around until they fall into place."

"But if I understood you correctly you're setting Meigs aside."

"This isn't about Meigs," I said.

"It's a way of staying connected though, isn't it?" He cleared his throat. "Our time is up for today."

Then Dr. Goldman stood up and reminded me that he'd be off both next week and the week between Christmas and New Year's, though why a Jewish man needed to take off Christmas Eve and then take a Christmas vacation was beyond me. I felt a surge of irritation, remembering how I'd often suspected him of siding with Mark because of their common religion. Not that he said anything outright, of course. But he could do a lot with a well-placed silence and those eyebrows.

CHAPTER 11

I checked my phone for messages as soon as I stepped out of the building. My noon appointment had canceled, leaving a good hour and a half free. Not enough time to get home for a nap, but too much to moon around the office waiting for the last appointment of the day. I tipped my face up to the sun. For the first time in ten days, being outdoors actually felt pleasant.

I walked to Clark's Dairy Restaurant, wedged in next to Clark's Pizza, halfway between my office and Yale. I slid onto one of the stools at the counter and ordered a bowl of split pea soup and a chocolate milkshake. Something I'd read recently had advised against eating dairy products while suffering with a cold — something about increasing mucus. Right now, though, comfort took priority, damn the consequences. When the soup was delivered, I crushed a package of Saltines over the top and began to eat. I blew on each steaming spoonful, thinking about church secrets, whatever they might be. Both Reverend Wesley and Paul were acting weird. And not just the kind of strange that might naturally follow a parishioner's unexpected death.

It occurred to me that Paul Cashman's apartment was only blocks away. We'd chatted about the Orange Street neighborhood — in coffee hour, of course — when he began his internship at our church.

I signaled the waitress and asked her to add a take-out carton of chicken noodle soup to my order. Soup in hand, I headed down Whitney Avenue toward Lawrence, savoring the last of my milkshake. It was rude not to call ahead — that's how I'd feel if someone just dropped in. But I had questions that couldn't be asked in front of the committee. And I suspected I'd get better answers if I took him by surprise. Number thirty-six Lawrence was an old Victorian mansion. I leaned hard on the door buzzer hand-lettered with Paul's name. After a short wait, his voice floated out from the intercom.

"Yes?"

"It's Rebecca Butterman. I took the chance of stopping by with some soup. May I come in for a minute?"

A long hesitation, then: "Second floor, door on the right. I'm not really in shape for company."

"I'll just drop this off — I won't stay." The buzzer sounded. I pushed open the door, went into the musty vestibule, and trooped up stairs covered with a shabby runner pinned down by brass bars. This had been someone's home once, now chopped into student apartments and let go like a tired old woman.

Paul cracked his door open and peeked out. I held out the soup with a cheery hello. He waited a beat, then moved aside and let me in. His face was the color of skim milk, almost matching the bandage on his forehead. He wore a bathrobe layered over a white T-shirt and jeans. Unshaven and slightly greasy, he looked like he hadn't bathed since arriving home from the hospital. It had not been a good week for clergy. Not the Congregational kind anyway.

"Sorry about this." He gestured at himself. "I wasn't expecting company."

"I know I'll see you tonight, but I was in the neighborhood and wanted to be sure you're doing okay. I feel a little bit responsible." I patted my widow's peak.

"Not your fault at all," he said with a wan smile. He set the container of soup on a

161

counter alongside his laptop and a stack of newspapers. "I'm glad I was there to break your fall."

"Full-service ministry," I said with one of Reverend Leo's phony chuckles, and waited.

"Can I make you a cup of tea or something?" Paul asked. A reluctant invitation, one I would usually be polite enough to turn down.

"If you don't mind, that sounds wonderful. I seem to have come down with a little cold and I still have one patient to see. Not to mention an interview with a very promising ministerial candidate." I grinned. "Tea would be just the thing to tide me over."

He sighed and cleared the loose papers off his tiny kitchen table. "Sit, sit." I settled into the chair against the wall, where the top rung had worn the fuzz off the flocked wallpaper, and shrugged my coat off. He filled the teakettle and went to his cupboard. "Red Zinger? Decaf green tea? Plain old Lipton's?"

"Definitely caffeine." I smiled again.

He draped tea bags into white mugs inscribed in blue script with "God is still speaking." Hadn't this been the motto for the campaign to include nontraditional members in the church?

I pointed to the cups. "Have you found

our congregation to be receptive to the Open and Affirming issue?" I asked. Opening and Affirming was shorthand for welcoming people of all sexual orientations and differing abilities into the Congregational Church. Each individual congregation has the choice of ratifying the concept. At best, ours was circling around the prospect of even a preliminary discussion.

"Mixed reactions." He shrugged. "Most folks who live out in the suburbs can't believe it applies to them. They don't believe they know any homosexuals, and they certainly can't understand why such a person would want to join our church."

"What do you think?" I asked.

Paul turned back to the stove to shift the whistling kettle off the flame. "In my mind, the principle is important, whether it applies to our people or not. But Reverend Wesley doesn't feel like the time is right," he said. "There are plenty of other problems that concern the entire congregation. And Wesley thinks we're better off waiting to raise controversial issues until I move into the assistant pastor position." His face colored a splotchy pink. "I mean, if I'm chosen. What I mean is, whoever is chosen should be involved in making that kind of decision. It's been known to splinter a

163

congregation." He poured boiling water into the mugs. "Honey? Sugar?"

"Honey sounds good."

He rustled through the cabinet next to the stove and came up with a plastic bear half full of crystallized honey. "I'm sorry," he stammered. "I don't at all mean to imply that I'm the committee's choice. Although I love your church and I would be very grateful for the opportunity to serve."

Looking half dead with embarrassment, he deposited a steaming mug in front of me, gripped the table, and leaned forward. "I wouldn't say it to anyone else, but if this position doesn't come through, I will be disappointed. If you've worked with a congregation for half a year and they don't like you enough to hire you, then where do you go?" He sucked in some air and collapsed into his seat. The tea sloshed over the edge of his mug and began to seep into his paper napkin. "I'm sorry, I shouldn't have said that."

I made a zipping motion over my lips and then smiled. "We'd be lucky to have you. But I'm sure the committee will consider all the variables and do what's right for the church. I'm there more or less for emotional support — Lacy's death was such a shock." I shook my head. "So sad. And scary."

He nodded vigorously.

"Speaking of scary, any ideas about what happened to you Saturday night?"

"Not really," he said. He patted his lips with the napkin, though he hadn't taken a drink. "Not really."

"Do you think someone spread that grease hoping you would fall?"

Paul hunched his shoulders, hooked his hands over his biceps, and shook his head. "A few of the parishioners aren't what you'd call warm, but geez, this is a church." His face paled even more, erupting with freckles of sweat.

"When I fell on you the other night, you said something before you passed out. You said Reverend Wesley was going somewhere?"

He turned his palms up and shrugged again. "I have no idea. I was pretty loopy — maybe deep down, I'm worried about his next vacation?" The colored blotches rushed back to mottle his skin.

"You did get a good knock on the noggin," I said, reaching to pat his hand. "Wesley's had a terribly stressful time this fall. How would you say he's been holding up?"

Paul flushed a third time. Anyone could read him like a book. A minister should be able to hold his counsel, not broadcast it when he's horrified or distressed. Right now Paul couldn't. And he was both.

"He'll be okay, once he has some steady help. The ladies in the office are very kind. The women behind every man and all that." He grinned.

I glanced at my watch. "I better hustle. I have a two o'clock waiting for me. Thanks for the tea. I'll see you tonight."

I trotted back to my office, reviewing the conversation and wondering what he'd started to tell me in the stairwell. Something he wasn't comfortable disclosing now. *Reverend Wesley is going . . . where?* Ridiculous. There was no way to guess.

I did give Paul credit for treating me like a normal person, not just sucking up. Like Ellen, he seemed to want the position badly. He seemed to think Reverend Wesley was his biggest supporter. And he'd be very disappointed if he wasn't hired.

Oh Lord, was *he* the one involved with Wesley?

CHAPTER 12

After finishing with my two o'clock, a Yale student panicked and depressed at the thought of going home for the holidays, I only wanted to collapse in bed. I promised myself a nap after making the reference calls the committee was expecting.

First up, Ellen Dark. I dialed the number of the Barstow Congregational Church in New Hampshire to talk to our former assistant minister.

"This is Dr. Rebecca Butterman. Might I speak with the Reverend Leo Sweeney?"

"You're in luck," said a cheerful female voice. "He's on his way in from lunch."

"Dr. Butterman, how are you?" Leo's voice was warm as an August morning, just as I remembered. Whether he truly cared a whit about speaking with me, I was meant to feel chosen. "Did you ever find the condo of your dreams?"

A question that showed why he was so

167

good at his job: He could distill a three-minute conversation held six months ago into the essence of what mattered.

"Right in Guilford," I said. "A stone's throw from the town dock. I have a front-row seat for ospreys, bluefish, even a red-tailed hawk from time to time."

"Sounds perfect," he said. "We heard a bit about the trouble you've had down there. Awfully sorry about Lacy Bailes. At a time like this, I can't help feeling like I left you all in the lurch. If you can think of anything I can do to help . . . Is it true that she was poisoned?"

"It's been a terrible shock all around," I agreed, ignoring the poison question. "Did you know her well?"

"How well is well?" asked Leo, but went on without waiting for an answer. "For a while last fall she chaired the stewardship committee: We teased her that our theme was shaming members into giving. Only she wasn't joking.

"She pushed hard to hold an all-church canvass at the end of the annual fund-raiser, phoning every person who hadn't pledged. And she wanted this done by the ministers." He chuckled. "Nightmarish logistics aside, can you imagine Wesley knocking on doors and asking for money?" Another robust chuckle. "Poor Wesley. Lacy hammered away at him until I finally had to step in and explain that we didn't have the time to go house-to-house to five hundred members. We wouldn't be able to visit the sick, attend any other meetings, or write our sermons. Though maybe those wouldn't be missed."

I laughed politely. "So she backed off?"

"She did. But only after I leveled with her that it wasn't going to happen. She was full of ideas and plans and energy, but not always what you'd call a team player. Terrible shame though. Tragic to see a life ended that way."

"It sure is. I understand she was very active in Alcoholics Anonymous," I said. "She helped a lot of people by being so open about it."

"I wasn't around before she got sober but I understand she was hell on wheels," said Leo. "I admire anyone who can pull herself out of a situation like that and then reach back to help the next guy in line." He made a clucking noise, like a hungry chicken. "But I don't have to tell you that the biggest obstacle in that disease is denial."

"Right." I'd want to remember not to tell him anything in confidence. "Umm, you're probably wondering why I'm calling. I'm

Lacy's replacement on the search committee. Either she didn't check the candidates'
references the way she promised or we can't
find her notes. Did she happen to call you
about the Reverend Ellen Dark? We don't
even know where to start."

"Oh Ellie, absolutely. I did speak briefly
with Lacy about her application. She's the
assistant at the little church two towns over,
so I hear all about her projects." He cleared
his throat. "People up here love Ellie. She's
nurturing without being smothering. She
works hard — like with Lacy, you'll have to
figure out a way to channel all that energy.
I'm very fond of Ellen."

"You've known her since divinity school,
right? What about her husband, will he have
trouble making a move like this?"

"No trouble with Harry. He's ten years or
so older than Ellen and he has a lot of
solitary interests. He can do them just as
well in Connecticut as New Hampshire.
Most spouses understand the drill when
they marry a minister. It's like the military
or foreign service — the moves come with
the job."

"How are your wife and babies?" I asked,
suddenly remembering Reverend Leo's wife
enormous with child at his going-away
party. She was a small woman who seemed

overwhelmed by the last weeks of her pregnancy — ankles swollen, face puffy, smudged raccoon eyes. How hard it must have been to be packing and moving just before giving birth to twins. She'd shown up and done her duty, but her heart wasn't in it.

"The kids are a joy," said Reverend Leo. "And my Daria's a trooper. I'd whip out the wallet photos if we weren't on the phone." His laugh was hearty and warm. And starting to get on my nerves.

"I'd love to see them sometime. Does Daria enjoy being a minister's wife?"

"She's an angel. But then, she knows how to pace herself: She's choosy about where and how much to get involved. And now that she has two kids and a job to keep her busy, she's pretty much a homebody."

"Not like Wesley's Beverly," I said.

He sighed. "Beverly struggled. She talked with me a bit, you know, before she left. Confidentially, of course."

"Of course," I said. And waited.

"Poor Bev. I wonder where she is?" He sighed again, more dramatically this time. "How's poor Paul holding up?"

"He was handling things rather nicely," I said, "up until he fell down the stairs the other night. The committee's interviewing him tonight." I forced a chuckle. "We hope his brains aren't addled by the tumble."

"He fell down the stairs?"

Should I tell him about the Crisco? I supposed it didn't much matter. Enough folks had been on the scene that the news would have already spread through Guilford and started up the interstate toward New Hampshire. I described what had happened.

"Paul's all right now. He'll be fine, really. It was just a slight concussion. The police are investigating," I added, whether they were or they weren't.

"Who would do something like that to Paul?" Leo exclaimed.

"We don't know what happened yet."

"Give him my best. I know Wesley thinks a lot of him." There was a pause. "Maybe I shouldn't mention this . . ."

"Oh please," I said. "It's too important to hold anything back."

"Nothing dramatic," he assured me. "And I don't know Paul that well. But the few weeks we overlapped, he seemed quite frail. Emotionally, that is."

"In what way?"

"Between us, when one of our youth members was questioning whether to become sexually active this past summer, he went to talk to Paul. Paul explored the pros

172

and cons with him in a — well — noncommittal way. The kid's parents found out and went crazy. Why do we want this kind of influence on our kids and he should be talking to my child about abstinence and look at the way the Catholic Church has handled things and blah, blah, blah. Paul froze. I happened to be in the hallway when I heard them yelling, so I was able to step in and help sort things out." He cleared his throat. "No doubt Paul will grow into the position if you hire him, but I found him a little green and rough around the edges."

"I appreciate your candor," I said.

"I've got a meeting to get to. As you know perfectly well, we can't make a decision in the church until we've talked it over ad nauseam and changed our minds a couple times." He laughed again. "Even with all that, we manage to table our motions about fifty percent of the time."

"Thanks for all your help. We'll keep you posted about Reverend Dark."

"Reverend Dark." He chuckled. "Unfortunate name for a minister. You all take care down there. I'm keeping you in my prayers, especially poor Paul." I heard the click of the line disconnecting.

I hung up and glanced over the notes I'd jotted. They didn't amount to much. Lacy as jackhammer. Poor Wesley. Poor Bev. Poor frozen Paul. Unfortunate name. Fond of Ellen.

Fond. I hate that word. Near the end of my marriage, I'd been masochistic enough to ask Mark if he still loved me. It felt like eons before he answered.

"I'm very fond of you."

The memory still rankled.

So did Leo really like Ellen or was this a tepid review cloaked in ministerial politeness? Not enough information — we'd simply have to ask Ellen who else was on her reference list and then see if their assessments agreed.

I put my head down on the desk and closed my eyes. What I'd give for a blank calendar the rest of the day. I almost drifted off to sleep, but the details of the visit with Paul Cashman kept spinning through my mind.

Reverend Wesley had touted him from the start of the search process as the correct candidate. And from what I could tell, Lacy had intended to block his nomination. And Paul had come right out and told me he didn't know what he'd do if he didn't get the job.

Even though Leo clearly didn't believe he could handle it. Was Leo jealous? But why would he be envious of the intern when he'd chosen to leave our church?

And Paul, what he was hiding? Something was off. Was he too nice? Too accommodating? Leo described him as frail, but I didn't really see that. I dialed Annabelle's office, hoping to catch her in between patients and tap into her knowledge and network at the Yale Divinity School.

"Hey," I said when she answered. "No customers working the sand trays this afternoon?"

She sighed. "I have one coming up in a few. How are things going?"

"I need your advice. Ministers again. The search committee is interviewing a divinity school intern tonight. I think he's lying about something, but I'm not sure what." I described Paul's nervousness at the church supper Saturday night, along with the Crisco accident, and his reaction to my visit. "If he's got a serious emotional problem, we'd sure like to know about it before offering him the job."

The phone crackled and I could hear Annabelle breathing. "As I think I told you at lunch, it's unlikely someone could get this far along in the process and be clinically disturbed. If something's wrong, psychologically speaking, it's going to be subtle. These candidates go through so much to get to the end point of actually serving in the ministry — clinical pastoral education, psychiatric evaluation, extensive supervision. Any major problems are picked up along the way and those folks are weeded out. It's not like the old days when candidates had one interview before they were released into the world."

My mind clicked into gear. "Psychiatric evaluation? Does that include psychological testing? Any chance you could convince someone to leak me a few sentences about Paul's results? Then I can let the committee know he's solid."

"Nil," she said firmly. "Forget it. Just do your job and stay out of trouble. Promise?"

I crossed my fingers. "Promise," I said.

"Gotta go — my patient's here."

My cell phone chirped as soon as I hung up.

Meigs sounded terse and imperious, per usual. "Can you stop by the station on the way home from work?"

He'd see me with a red nose and puffy eyes. I squashed that thought: Forget it.

"I'm just leaving New Haven. I'll be there in half an hour."

The temperature had dropped enough since lunch for the slushy roads to glaze over into sheets of ice. I edged onto the highway, guided my Honda into the slow lane, and crept home. Just off my exit, a cruiser with lights flashing was parked diagonally across the road, reducing the flow of traffic to a crawl. A maroon minivan had spun off the road at the intersection and crashed into a pickup truck, leaving metal strewn across the pavement. A policeman dressed in a heavy overcoat and a hat with earflaps waved me around a chunk of debris. He appeared to be pointing to the left lane. I pulled over. Now jabbing his gloved finger at me, the cop waved frantically for me to stop. I rolled my window down, wincing at the blast of cold air. He filled the frame of my window, frost in his mustache and an angry look on his face.

"Do you normally drive on the left side of the road?" he bellowed, voice belligerent and humorless.

I felt my face flush. "Sorry, Officer. It was a little confusing."

"Confusing?" he said. "Did I indicate that you should be driving on the left?"

Very close to tears, I looked for a way to explain. What would satisfy him? Nothing. The answer he wanted was "No."

"I'm sorry, Officer, I made a mistake."

"You sure did." He glared. "Watch where

you're going next time."

By the time I'd driven the last mile to the police station, I'd moved past humiliated and scared into boiling mad.

"I'm here for Detective Meigs," I snapped at the receptionist.

Meigs found me pacing the waiting area and escorted me to his office.

"Good evening." He smiled and pointed to the visitor's chair.

Another pointing cop. Without sitting or answering his greeting, I lashed out.

"No wonder people don't trust the cops! They're assholes."

"Excuse me?"

"You heard me." I crossed my arms over my chest, began to cough, and sank into the chair, groping in my pocket for a Kleenex.

He scratched his head and perched on the corner of the desk. "Would you like to talk about it?"

"Not really." I took a deep breath and broke into more spasms of coughing.

"I'll get you some water." He strode past me into the hall. I dug around in the depths of my purse and came up with a sugar-free mint. A bottom-feeder, prehistoric from the looks of the wrapper. I wiped my eyes and blew my nose.

By the time Meigs returned with water in

a paper cone, I was feeling a little calmer, even sheepish about attacking him. He was a cop after all, what did I expect? I explained what had happened on the way over.

"He could have corrected me without being nasty."

"Sounds like Kramer," Meigs said. "He can be a little crabby."

My shoulders stiffened. "No," I said, wagging my finger. "This wasn't *crabby,* it was *nasty.* And I'm a reasonable human being. Trust me, I wasn't being rude."

He raised his eyebrows.

I felt the tide of rage start to rise again. "Don't you understand? People are afraid of cops. An experience like this makes it worse. You can buy all the publicity you want in the *Shoreline Times* about friendly police-citizen relations, but it basically boils down to bullshit. That's *B-U-L-L* bullshit." I was breathing hard and I could practically feel my eyes bulging. "And why the hell would you take a job like this anyway, working with jerks like him?"

He tipped his head, the tiniest smile edging onto his lips, which only made me madder.

"No really," I insisted, "what could possibly turn you on about all this?" I flung my hands out and banged my fingers on the sharp edge of his desk. Tears sprang to my eyes. "*Ow!* Dammit!"

"Because there are bad people out there doing bad things to good people," he said.

I stood up. "I got confused about his lousy directions and I'm a bad person?"

He wasn't smiling now. "He didn't know who or what you were. He was doing his job."

"Then you do your own goddamn detective work." I shrugged into my coat and snatched up my purse. Meigs came around the desk and grabbed my arm before I could storm out.

"Look, I'm not saying we're all perfect. Sure, we have some assholes on power trips."

I looked down at his large fingers gripping my arm. His nails were slightly jagged, bitten down even with the quick. He let go and took a step back. "Between us, we're keeping an eye on Kramer, okay?" he said.

I felt the anger begin to fade.

"Do me a favor," he said. "Let's start over. Sit down and tell me about the meetings you've had so far."

I sat, knowing I'd overreacted. A little bit. Probably related to the session with Dr. Goldman. I blew my nose again — congested from the tears and the coughing —

and described the committee's interview with Ellen Dark.

"She thinks she's a shoo-in. I'm wondering if Lacy told her that. We can't find any notes from previous meetings or calls Lacy made to references. Mrs. McCabe — the sexton's wife, she's filling in for our regular secretary — is making a more thorough search." I looped my hair behind one ear. It felt limp and slightly greasy. "I had a little chat with Paul Cashman this afternoon."

Meigs uncrossed his legs and put both hands on the desk.

"He's a nice guy, he really is. He did say he'll be very disappointed if he doesn't get this job."

Meigs frowned. "I don't want you conducting interviews outside the purview of the committee meetings. Just your observations, that's it. I thought I'd made that clear."

I pulled my coat around my shoulders, forcing myself to stay put, not pop up again like a startled rabbit. "I left several messages and didn't hear anything back from you. From the looks of it, the police weren't doing squat."

"Just because I'm not reporting to you doesn't mean we aren't working on the case." Meigs sighed and ran his hand over his face. "The tox screen on the victim came back testing positive for glycosides. That's poison," he said. "Which pretty much rules out a heart attack. They're doing more tests to narrow it down, but we should have the search warrant later today."

"And all this means what?" I asked, feeling leaden and weak.

"You tell me," he said. "We're interviewing some of your Women's League members to see who heard the poison lady's presentation."

"You really think one of our church ladies murdered Lacy Bailes?"

Meigs leaned back in his desk chair, balancing on two legs, and tugged on his ear. "Reverend Wesley refuses to say why he went to Lacy's house on Friday night."

"So he's still a suspect?" Surely they could find someone more likely than Reverend Wesley.

He just looked at me for a moment. "A guy turns up on the scene with a dead lady and no decent explanation, we're going to look him over damn carefully." The chair legs banged back to the floor. "Whether he's a minister or whether he isn't."

CHAPTER 13

Once home, I went directly to bed and slept hard for forty-five minutes. I woke up feeling groggy, congested, and depressed — not at all interested in another committee meeting. I rustled through the freezer and extracted a Tupperware of lentil soup from the back corner. Not my favorite: After the stress of last summer's move, I'd tried to counteract too many fast-food meals with a "pack as many superfoods into the dish as possible" phase. Meaning the soup was heavy on kale and flaxseed and low on taste. I lifted the lid and saw the telltale pebbling of freezer burn across the top. But I was starving and running late so I slid the container into the microwave and popped a leek biscuit from Four and Twenty Blackbirds Bakery into the toaster oven. Then I opened a can of Friskies for Spencer and headed into the bathroom to wash my face. The face peering back from the mirror looked positively ghoulish — a white cast, dark circles under both eyes, and a red and chapped nose and upper lip. Nothing concealer and blush could even begin to disguise. I patted moisturizer on the chapped skin, considered adding eye makeup, then quickly ruled it out. My nose was running like a leaky faucet in spite of more pseudoephedrine than any reasonable manufacturer would recommend. Black streaks would not improve the look.

A burning smell wafted in from the kitchen. I dashed in and yanked the biscuit from the toaster with an oven mitt. The top layer was incinerated. And the lentil soup looked no more appealing warm than it had frozen. I trimmed the top of the biscuit off, slathered it with butter and honey, and wolfed it down leaning over the sink.

Lights twinkled in the windows of the condo next door, a dazzle of red, green, and white. The holiday lighting warden, Mrs. Dunbarton, must have a coronary every time she walked by. The new neighbors, a retired couple still devoted after forty years of the "ole ball and chain" (as they told every person they met), had a decidedly more buoyant outlook than my deceased neighbor, Madeline. They'd already invited the entire complex to a cookie swap and grab-bag gift exchange later in the week. I remembered with a stab of dread that I'd drawn Mrs. Dunbarton's name. Was there a gift shop on the Guilford green that specialized in sourpuss dowagers?

I wiped my lips and hands on a green checkered dish towel and grabbed my purse.

"Send out the dogs if I'm not home by nine," I told Spencer. It was unmistakable — he frowned.

The rest of the search committee and Paul had already gathered in the parlor by the time I arrived. Paul looked much better than when I'd seen him earlier in the day, showered and shaved, shiny brown hair lapping over the Band-Aid at his hairline. He wore a gray suit, white dress shirt, and a plaid tie in muted Christmas colors.

"Good evening, everyone!" I said, trying for a cheerfulness I didn't feel.

Barney Brooks started in before I even sat down. "Since we all know each other, superficially at least, I thought we might have a different — a deeper — kind of discussion tonight." He glanced around the room and without giving the rest of us time to react, turned to Paul. "Can you tell us about the circumstances of your call?"

Paul shifted and gulped, mouth working.

He looked like a fish on the beach.

Nice icebreaker, Barney. "Deep breath," I suggested with a friendly smile. I leaned back into the wing chair, plucking at the frayed fabric on the armrest, all hopes for a painless yet productive meeting ebbing away.

Paul pinned his lips into a grimace, air whistling between his teeth. "It's not a dramatic story," he said. "I always thought I'd be a doctor like my dad. But during college breaks, I began to talk with my hometown pastor about whether I should be saving souls rather than bodies." He grinned.

Barney narrowed his eyes. "That's it?"

Paul uncrossed his legs and swallowed. "I didn't have an 'aha!' moment, if that's what you're asking. My sense of belonging in the ministry has evolved; I know it's a good direction — I've felt so comfortable here this year."

Not entirely true, according to my earlier conversation with Reverend Leo.

"And my work with the youth has been an unexpected pleasure."

"In other words, you stumbled into this," Barney said.

Paul looked stunned — he did the gasping fish thing again. I had a strong urge to bail him out, but I held back. He'd need to

186

handle worse pressure than this if he was offered the position. For starters, a congregational meeting — held to approve major church decisions such as hiring a new minister — could resemble a pit of mixed piranhas and sharks.

"That isn't what the young man said," Mrs. Wiggett sputtered.

"He said it was an evolution," Babette piped up in a trembling voice.

Paul nodded gratefully. "Not everyone takes a direct route, but the destination may be the same."

"How would you handle a parent's concern that a homosexual was advising his or her child?" Barney asked.

"For God's sake," yelped Mrs. Wiggett. "You're way out of line!"

But Paul leaned forward earnestly and began to talk. "As you might imagine, we discussed this issue in some depth in divinity school. *God is still speaking* — that's what our denomination's motto says. But speaking through actions not words. Most parents hope for wisdom and stability in their children's mentors. That's certainly what I'll try to provide."

He was beginning to sound like a minister. Though he hadn't really answered the question.

Finally we pressed on to the issues we'd planned to discuss — how he anticipated handling moving from student to leader within the congregation, what ideas he had for attracting youth to the church programs, and his five- and ten-year goals. It was almost nine and I was exhausted.

At the first fault line in the conversation, I inserted myself. "We appreciate you coming in tonight so soon after your fall. It's been a difficult week for all of us. Add a concussion . . ." I shook my head. "Well, you're a trooper."

Paul stood to thank us and shook each committee member's hand. "If you have any more questions, you know where to find me." He smiled and left, closing the door gently behind him.

"What the hell is the matter with you?" Mrs. Wiggett asked Barney. She was bristling on the couch, a dogfight in the making.

I jumped in again. "I know we have a lot to discuss," I said, "but I'm not feeling well. Could we possibly meet tomorrow after the funeral reception to hash everything out?"

"It won't hurt us to sleep on it," agreed Babette. "At least I don't think so?"

I wished them a good night and went down the hallway to the church office to make copies of my notes. Best if everyone on the committee was starting with the same facts tomorrow — right in front of their eyes. My head ached just thinking about it. Reverend Wesley's door was open a crack, spilling light into the room. He appeared in his doorway, wringing his hands.

"How did everything go? Did Paul do all right?"

"He held up fairly well, considering Barney," I said, wondering whether to pin Wesley down right now about Paul. I was too tired to take it on.

"Crap," said Reverend Wesley, scowling. "He's an idiot. What is the matter with that man?" He looked at me, suddenly seeming to realize I didn't look well. "Shouldn't you be home in bed?"

Of course I should be home in bed. I had moved beyond crabby into put-upon territory, my eyes and nose swollen and sore and a full-bore sinus headache beginning to throb.

"I need to run off copies of tonight's minutes and the notes I took this afternoon when I phoned the candidates' references. We couldn't find a thing from Lacy — and I know she spoke with Reverend Leo. He told me so this afternoon."

"Leo, how is he?" he asked, straightening

his tie and buttoning his sweater — an old-fashioned tan wool cardigan like my grand-father used to wear. "Lacy did keep careful notes — I saw her paperwork on Nancy's desk, waiting in the typing queue."

"Mrs. McCabe doesn't remember seeing anything from Lacy."

He coughed into a white hankie. "I'm sure Nancy could put her hands right on the notes, but I'm not going to bother her when her mother's gravely ill. We'll ask when she returns to work. From the sound of things, that might be after Christmas. You'll just have to proceed without them."

"Fine," I snapped. "We'll do what we can. But I don't even know who else to call. It looks very unprofessional to have to ask your candidates for their materials a second time. We're meeting again tomorrow," I added, staring right at him. "Honestly, I think it would be better if you weren't there for this discussion. Everyone knows how you feel and tempers are short."

He sighed. "I guess I've pressed them pretty hard."

An opening. "With so much going on — Lacy's murder and the holidays — wouldn't it be better if we took a little time off and got back to this after New Year's?"

"Not acceptable," he said.

"But why?"

He pursed his lips. "We've dragged through this long enough. We have two well-qualified candidates. Paul, in fact, has worked with us for six months. If your committee can't make a decision —" He shook his head. "It's not fair to the congregation to have a couple of nincompoops hijack the process."

I hid a smile. Hadn't heard that word used outside Brittany's circle.

"How're you feeling about handling Lacy's funeral?" I asked. Hard to picture him conducting her service when he seemed to be a suspect in her murder. It just plain looked bad. And wouldn't her family object?

"I'm feeling fine. But in any case, Reverend Chanton is taking the lead."

I retrieved the papers from the copy machine, considering whether to push him for more details about Friday night. Whether or not Meigs wanted me meddling, I was the one with the best access to Reverend Wesley. I tucked the copies into my purse and turned to face him.

"Listen, Wes, I know this isn't easy, but will you tell me why you were at Lacy's house the night she died?"

Expressions crossed his face like fast-moving clouds. He pursed his lips again and drew his eyebrows together. "I wanted to get her support. For Paul. She'd never given him a proper chance. She made her mind up before even looking over his materials. She was going to sit through his interview, but she might as well have put plugs in her ears. And then she poisoned Barney Brooks."

"She . . . *poisoned* Barney?"

"Metaphorically speaking, of course," he snapped.

"Of course." I tapped my head with my fingers. "Did Detective Meigs tell you that Lacy's tox screen came back positive? Poison," I said.

Wesley blanched.

"What exactly happened when you got to her house Friday night?"

His chin dropped to his chest. "I knocked; she didn't answer." He glanced back up. "I'd called ahead of course," he said through gritted teeth. "She was expecting me at eight or so. When she didn't answer, I got worried and went in." He shook his head. "This is ridiculous," he said. "I didn't kill her. They're on the wrong trail."

Wesley's phone rang. "Excuse me, please." He retreated to his office.

Remembering that I'd left my original notes in the copy machine, I turned back to remove them and switch the machine off. With Reverend Wesley still murmuring on his office phone, I turned out the lights, pulled the secretary's door closed, and left the building.

On the way to the car, I smelled smoke and recognized its origin almost instantly — the Alcoholics Anonymous group that met in the lower level of the building. The ban on indoor smoking in Connecticut means attendees gather outside the entrance to smoke and talk, even in subfreezing weather. I thought about going around the corner to mingle with the AA members. Not a chance in hell I'd blend in. And what would I ask anyway — was Lacy acting strange before she died?

I drove home — too exhausted and numb to think one more thought.

Pulling into the garage, I noticed a package sitting on top of my curbside *New York Times* delivery box. Substitute nincompoop mailman? Better pick it up tonight before it was blown away or soaked through by another couple inches of snow. I parked, flipped on the outside lights, and slogged down the driveway and across the grass. A loud popping noise broke the silence. I felt a whistle of air pass my cheek. Suddenly terrified, I dropped to my knees in the snow, breathing hard and heart hammering, pressed into the yoga child's pose, and listened.

Had it been a gunshot? I heard the distant sound of footsteps crunching on the frozen street. A car started up a few blocks over. I was shivering uncontrollably.

I crawled back across the lawn to the garage, ducked inside, and called 911.

"I'd like to report a possible gunshot," I told the dispatcher. "Maybe someone shot — at me." She took my address and promised to send someone over.

I poured myself an inch of Maker's Mark and huddled on the couch clutching Spencer. Minutes later, car doors slammed. I crossed the room and peered out the window. Meigs and a uniformed officer sprinted up the walk and banged my knocker.

I unlocked the door and recognized the second man as Kramer, the cop who'd yelled at me this afternoon. He smirked. I would not cry in front of this man.

"I believe someone might have shot at me," I said stiffly, fighting for composure, and described the noises at the mailbox, the possible crunching footsteps, the possible car.

"Lock the door," said Meigs. "We'll have

a look around outside."

I put water on for coffee and slid Emmy Lou Harris's Christmas album into the CD player. Maybe I could pretend I wasn't as terrified as I actually felt. Meigs returned ten minutes later without Kramer, but carrying a brown box.

"We didn't find anything," he said, stamping his feet on the mat. "This is what you went out for?"

I took the package from Meigs. A box from Orvis — probably the golf sweater I'd ordered for my brother-in-law. I sank to the sofa, the package in my lap.

"You say the noise sounded like a gun?" Meigs looked sympathetic.

"I don't have any experience with what guns sound like," I said, "except on TV. It was more the whistling." My hands started to shake again. "Coffee?" I asked brightly.

Meigs shook his head. "I'm going to post Kramer to patrol your neighborhood tonight. We'll look again in the daylight. Maybe you want to stay with a friend?"

I said the first thing that popped into my head. "I'll call Mark — my ex. He can sleep on the couch," I added, feeling the heat rush to my face and neck.

Meigs nodded curtly. "We'll talk tomorrow. But I'm taking you off the search committee."

"I don't believe that's your call." I glowered. I couldn't help myself — his pronouncements just rubbed the wrong way.

"Let us know if you have any more trouble." He wheeled around and stomped down the sidewalk as I slammed the door shut.

Why had I told him I would call Mark? There wasn't a chance in hell he'd come over. Nor that I'd ask. Imagine Kramer outside my house and Mark indoors . . . I'd never sleep. I shut off the teakettle and the music, checked the locks on the doors and windows one more time, and retreated to my room.

I collapsed in bed — my dream all day. Even with Spencer curled up between my legs, I felt wide-awake and tense. I was scared to death. The noise had to have been an illusion of my overstretched imagination. I lay in the dark, snuffling through my blocked nasal passages, pushing off thoughts about the imaginary gun and its owner. Finally, I snapped the light back on, lifted out my laptop from the nightstand drawer, and waited for the computer to boot up. I'd distract myself with something completely different: tracking down my father. Spencer stretched into a *C*-shape and then draped himself, rumbling, across my waist.

Once the software loaded, I typed his name — Arthur Butterman — into the Google search bar. I know remarkably little about him — haven't wanted to know. My grandparents, reserved Yankees who silently blamed him for their daughter's death, had been just as happy to let the "Arthur problem" lie. Hard for them not to pin their daughter's depression and subsequent suicide on this man they'd never liked much anyway. So if he moved a distance away and "forgot" to send for his own daughters during their court-ordered visitation, it was okay with them.

I knew Artie, as his friends called him, was a plant scientist who specialized in new varieties of peanuts. According to Janice during one of the few conversations we've had on the topic, that was where his troubles with my mother (the frustrated artist) began and ended.

"They didn't speak the same language," Janice had once said. "She was Sylvia Plath to his Albert Einstein. Only he wasn't all that smart." She sniffed. "Of course, I'm no expert in legal terminology, but Jim goes out of his way to explain his more interesting cases to me. And I tell him about my day. Even the little things are important, Rebecca. He misses a lot of time with Brittany and so he appreciates that I fill him in. It's all about communication," she said smugly.

Thank you, Ann Landers, I'd wanted to say.

The Google search loaded with dozens of links to papers on the development of non-allergenic peanuts, most generated from Michigan State University. I clicked on the icon for his E-mail and composed a short note.

Dear Arthur: As your daughter by name and biology —

Delete. This was going to be harder than I'd thought. I tried again.

Dear Arthur: I have some questions about our family's medical history (your side) and would appreciate it if we could be in touch. No hurry.

Happy holidays,
Dr. Rebecca Butterman

Couldn't get much more noncommittal and cool than that. I sent it off. We could get into the angst and castigation in person.

An E-mail chimed its arrival. It was from Angie, the subject line: "Bob." Damn.

Bob tells me he hasn't heard from you. How the hell are you going to land a man if you won't call him back?

The second E-mail, from Jillian at *Bloom!* was almost as bad.

Rebecca, darling, did you get my message? I was expecting your holiday advice column today. We go live with the issue on Friday. And though you are always brilliant, I would like some time to look it over. Call me in the morning if there's a problem.

And then a third E-mail arrived, from Dr. Art Butterman at MSU. Fingers trembling, I clicked on it.

This message is an autoreply generated by MSU list management. Dr. Butterman is on sabbatical in Thailand until spring. Emergencies should be directed to Mrs. Tina Gerrity, department secretary.

I blew out a sigh of relief. Speaking with my father was long past emergency status.

I set the alarm for six, put the computer to sleep, and turned out the light. Punching my pillow flat, I turned restlessly, legs tangling in my flannel nightgown. I got up again and took two NyQuil tablets, then layered a second pillow over the first to raise my head a few inches and give myself a chance to breathe.

Half an hour later, I was still wide-awake and miserable. My brain whirled with images of my parents — young, of course, because that was the only way I'd known them — and questions about Lacy's death.

Who would show for her funeral tomorrow? For my mother, the church had been packed with shocked and curious acquaintances. Standing room only for the young woman who'd appeared normal in the grocery store and at the PTA, but who'd been desperate enough to take her life and leave her daughters. Mostly I remembered pressing against my grandmother in the pew, her body smelling faintly of lemon. And stiff with the weight of bewildering grief and no release valve, I realized later.

Crap, as Reverend Wesley would say. I rolled the snoring cat off my stomach, turned the light and the computer on again, and began to write a note for Dr. Aster, not even checking the letters from readers. This time I'd make one up.

Dear Dr. Aster:
My girlfriend's father passed away last week. I only knew him through her stories — not nice ones, I might add. They did not have a close relationship. Am I obligated to attend the funeral? If so, what do I do about condolences for a man who really rates nothing more than good riddance?

Yours truly,
Muddled in Milwaukee

Dear Muddled:
Most people attend funerals for these reasons: (1) to celebrate the life of the person who died, (2) to ease along their own grieving process, and (3) to show support for the survivors.

Since you didn't know your friend's father, you'll be concentrating on number three. Whether or not they were close, she will appreciate your presence. Relationships with our parents are so seldom black-and-white: She may very well find she feels more than she expected. These

feelings of loss might be related to the relationship she wished she had with her father, not the less desirable reality.

What to say to your friend? Stick with something simple like, "I'm here if you need me." And then make that come alive. Good luck and be thoughtful!

Not exactly a holiday theme, but if Jillian was busy enough, maybe she wouldn't notice. I added this question to the file containing my advice about the wicked stepmother and the column about how to handle a split from your husband at Christmas, and sent it off to *Bloom!* This time when I shut the light off, mercifully, sleep came.

CHAPTER 14

The alarm shrilled painfully. I didn't dare
hit the *snooze* button: I'd crowded my first
three patients into the early morning hours
so I could attend Lacy's funeral. After a hot
shower and a cup of coffee, I performed a
quick body scan: My headache had lifted,
my breathing was coming easier, my ankle
felt almost normal. I glanced at my watch.
Breakfast would have to be a bagel and
follow-up coffee from the drive-thru window
at Dunkin' Donuts, gulped on the drive to
Orange Street.

My first patient, Ellison, rolled in at 7:45,
still no closer to having finished her dis-
sertation on young mothers whose children
demonstrated ambivalent emotional attachment than she had been the week before.
Sometimes I wanted to grab her shoulders,
shake her, and shriek: "For God's sake, just
write the damn thing!"

Instead we were working slowly through

203

the meaning of graduation, her accomplished family's heavy expectations, and her suspicion that a female with a PhD would be sunk in the man department. Would no-nonsense Dr. Aster help her more than I could? I reminded myself that the frustration I was feeling simply reflected hers.

Finally Ellison clattered down the back stairway. I scratched out a few notes about her session. What would Dr. Aster have told her? Set up goals — short and sweet. And follow up with positive reinforcement — dessert to reward writing a page, maybe a massage after finishing a chapter. I jotted down the bare bones of a *Bloom!* column on the subject of goals — remembering that several of my readers had asked about making New Year's resolutions. My cell phone vibrated. Meigs had left a message while I was with Ellison, inquiring how the night had gone.

"We took another look around. No sign of footprints or tire tracks that didn't belong, though that's a little unreliable with the icy conditions. And no bullet casings anywhere. Were you sure about what you heard?"

I wasn't sure at all. My nerves were jumpy and my ears were clogged by the head cold.

"The autopsy results are in," he continued. "And we've searched the victim's premises. Lily of the valley was used to poison Ms. Bailes's tea. And lily of the valley was one of the topics in the Poison Lady's presentation. Call me when you get a chance. I'm serious about wanting you to step down from your committee. For your own safety."

I was glad he was concerned, but I had to attend today's meeting. I shouldn't be a target in the parlor in broad daylight. Sounded like I wasn't a target last night either.

Jillian's voice was next. She was sorry to hear I was under the weather. Pre-Christmas germs notwithstanding, she wanted a replacement for the funeral etiquette Q and A, ASAP. Not that it wasn't perfectly well written and quite helpful, but she simply didn't see the holiday connection. "Maybe if it was Easter," she said with a giggle. "Sorry that was a joke. Not a very good one."

I called her back — hoping no self-respecting New York editor would be at her desk by 8:30 a.m. — and left a voicemail promising a substitute column by the end of the day.

My second patient leaned on the door buzzer as I was dialing Meigs's number. The cops would have to wait. I checked to be sure the ringer was on vibrate, slid the phone into the top desk drawer, and walked out to the waiting area. Rufus shuffled up the final step, head bowed, but not low enough to obscure the unhappy set of his mouth. I couldn't help wondering whether he might have been a more cheerful person with a change as small as a different name. Something manly and definitive, say Rob, or Mike, or Jack . . .

Flushing hotly, I wished him a good morning and ushered him into the office. We'd been talking about his marriage for the last three months — whether he should leave his wife, a dour woman who criticized him constantly, reminding him of his mother. Fifty minutes later, he exited with the same shuffle. Even in the face of no visible progress, his interior landscape could very well be shifting. Right.

I sighed and dialed Meigs, bracing for his gruff morning voice.

"Leave a message," his voicemail said.

"Rebecca Butterman here. I didn't get a chance to tell you, but last night's meeting was a little rough. Barney Brooks led a charge at Paul Cashman. We're meeting briefly after the funeral to process our impressions. I saw Reverend Wesley after the session. He swears he was at Lacy's to get her support for Paul. I know you don't want me conducting interviews, but I didn't see how it would hurt to ask. And I do plan to attend the meeting this afternoon. They need me to finish what they've started."

Just then my third patient announced her arrival with a series of buzzes. Beep, beep, beep, beep, beep . . . beep, beep. I pressed *end* and put the phone away. Let Meigs harangue me later.

The hour with Jeannette passed quickly. She adores the process of psychotherapy, unlike Rufus, who finds my attention and questions intrusive and annoying.

"I've made some decisions," she told me close to the end of the session. "I've cut my visit home over Christmas to three days rather than five."

I smiled. "Smart. It takes more than three for the usual family drama to unfold."

"Exactly!" she said. "And if I start to regress, the damage will be contained because I'm leaving the next day. I've talked to my sister and we've made a pact: We're not going to bring up Dad's drinking or how my mother lets him get away with murder."

"Christmas is stressful enough," I agreed. "I like your strategy. Just keep track of your reactions and feelings so we can continue to work on them when you get back in January. We'll see what worked and what pushed your buttons."

"Have a merry Christmas," she said, then blushed. "Or whatever you celebrate!"

"Thanks," I said, opening the double doors and watching her bob happily down the stairs. No doubt she'd be more subdued next visit, but she was young enough and smart enough to really learn from the process. I sighed. I wasn't always so sure about me. After turning down the heat and locking the doors, I set off for my car and Lacy's funeral.

Running late as usual, I parked alongside the Guilford town green, hoping my car wouldn't be sideswiped by a plow, and dashed up the salted walk to the church. The church bells were already ringing. A seat in the balcony would provide an optimal view of body language and faces, so I started up the steps. Mr. McCabe rushed past me, his shirt damp with sweat from hauling on the bell ropes. No windup electronic music for this church — we had three hundred years of history to uphold. I settled into a front pew.

A river of red poinsettias framed the curved stairs that led up to the pulpit.

Synthetic green wreaths with bright red bows hung on the walls down the length of the church and plug-in candles glowed in the wavy windowpanes. An enormous vase of lilies graced the communion table below the pulpit — for Lacy, I assumed — an odd juxtaposition of sadness and holiday celebration.

The organist finished a subdued rendition of Handel's *Messiah* and Reverend Chanton picked his way carefully up the stairs between the poinsettias to the pulpit. After an opening prayer, he said, "The book of Romans asks the question: *Who will separate us from the love of God?*"

Then he began to speak about the importance of purpose and purity in the Christian life. I looked at my watch. Seven minutes already and hardly any mention of Lacy. Had he even met the woman? Not that his homily didn't apply to Lacy, but when would he get to the personal reflection about the deceased that the bereaved expect? Reverend Wesley, seated below the pulpit near the lilies, looked glazed — worse than last night. His cough punctuated Reverend Chanton's words like a drumbeat, making my own throat itch.

The thoughts I'd been working to contain since last night seeped into my consciousness: It was becoming more and more clear that one of *us* had murdered Lacy. And spread the Crisco. And even possibly shot at me. I pressed my fingers to my temples and tried to concentrate on studying the mourners' expressions. There was a short row of what looked like family in the third pew. No one would sit that close to the front if they didn't have to, even the members who might have ordinarily staked their claim to those seats. Five or six dozen people were scattered in the pews behind them. No tears yet, but so far the minister hadn't given them much to work with.

I rolled my head from left to right and back again, easing out the tension. Was the killer right here in the meetinghouse? I shivered, trying to imagine how he or she might feel. Face it, we were all on edge, but imagine the murderer's perspective. How would it feel to participate in the activities of the Christmas season, trying to act normal, knowing the cops were on your tail? Had the killer been at the church supper? Did she sing in the choir or wear white gloves and ring one of the bells in the special holiday appearance of the handbell choir? Would his children perform in the pageant on Christmas Eve?

Maybe the killer felt calm after the murder

— like a troubled adolescent feels after self-cutting — almost as if the physical act of letting blood relieved the pressure of stoppered emotions. But maybe now his — or her — panic was rising, knowing the cops were drawing closer to a solution. If in fact they were.

It had to be someone Lacy knew. She was a sensible, ambitious single woman. She would not have asked a random stranger in for a cup of tea. And robbers don't read up on plant poisons. I shivered again. Chances were, it would be someone I knew too.

A bulletin from last Sunday's service had been shoved in the rack behind a hymnal. I pulled it out and leafed through the announcements, guiding my mind to another track. Jodi and Brook Jerzyk had donated the flowers for Sunday's service in celebration of twenty-five years of marriage. This couple doesn't look more than midforties, meaning they'd married by twenty-one. How had they ever pulled off staying together that long? I barely knew who I was at twenty-one, never mind agreeing to tether myself to a *boy* for life.

I read on.

The Advent dinner had been a big success, with enough "warm woolies" collected for seventy-three kids and adults. There were still a few spaces left on the tree in the fellowship hall — donations of hats, mittens, and gloves were welcome.

Pledge money was behind budget for December and members were reminded that church expenses continued even during the Christmas high season. And the junior and senior high youth groups were conducting a fund-raiser that involved a Christmas carol session for those "hard to buy for" on your list. Which brought to mind Mrs. Dunbarton. I tucked the bulletin into my purse.

Inviting Lacy's cousin, Dennis Spjut, to speak at the lower microphone, Reverend Chanton started down from the pulpit. Dennis came forward, dressed in a baggy blue suit, his balding head shining in the overhead spotlight.

"My mother was always close to Lacy's mother," he began. "We spent time at their Madison beach cottage every summer — crabbing, sunbathing, flying kites. I remember sunburn and jellyfish stings and way too much ice cream."

The congregation chuckled. You tend to get a generous audience at a funeral.

"I was quite sure that one day Lacy and I would be married." His voice broke and he flashed a smile at a woman in the front row.

His present wife, most likely. "Life is all about family and Lacy was part of ours. We shall miss her imposing presence." As he returned to his seat, I peered over the balcony rail to scan the back of the church for Meigs. No sign of him. Reverend Chanton shuffled back over to the microphone.

"Next, Lacy's friend Roger Kennedy will speak," he said, and stepped aside for a tall, skinny man who I immediately recognized as Santa's photographer at the church supper.

"Good morning," said Roger with a warm smile. "My name is Roger."

"Good morning, Roger," answered a smattering of mourners.

Alcoholics Anonymous, I thought. They begin every meeting with first-name-only greetings.

"Lacy was a good woman," he said, dabbing his cheeks with a folded handkerchief. "She had some rough times, but with the grace of God and Friends of Bill, she pulled herself out of it. And she was relentless about helping other people. She was blunt, she was persistent, she was funny. Every one of us could learn from her: Lacy Bailes knew how to *let go and let God.* She had *an attitude of gratitude.*"

As opposed to an attitude of platitudes, I

213

thought unkindly, glancing again at my watch. The short night was beginning to catch up with me. And so was my anxiety about the poisoning and the crazy prank on Paul. I pulled the bulletin back out of my purse and began to jot down a list for Meigs.

1. Individuals likely to have been at the church during the Poison Lady's presentation: Mrs. Wiggett, Mr. McCabe, Mrs. McCabe, Paul Cashman, Reverend Wesley, many other Women's League members. (Mrs. McCabe would be able to produce the luncheon roster.)
2. Individuals at the church supper: Mrs. Wiggett, Mr. McCabe, Mrs. McCabe, Paul Cashman, Barney Brooks, Roger Kennedy, many, many others. (There was a sign-up sheet, but it will only be approximate.)
3. Individuals I have spoken with about Lacy over the past few days: Paul Cashman, Reverend Wesley, Barney Brooks, Mrs. Wiggett, Mrs. McCabe, Babette Finster.

I skimmed the list for the most logical murder suspect. *Hopeless.*

"It's very hard for me to imagine anyone wanting to hurt Lacy," Roger said softly.

My thoughts exactly.

Then Roger laughed. "Though it isn't one bit hard to imagine being annoyed or angry with her. She took to heart the idea that she was put here to help other people and, by golly, she was going to do that, whether you wanted the help or whether you didn't." After offering a couple of vignettes and a short prayer, he surrendered the mike.

Reverend Wesley stood and moved to the podium. He cleared his throat several times and began to cough, finally sinking back down while waving apologetically at the congregation. After several minutes of uncomfortable silence, he surfaced again and offered a closing prayer, his cheeks red and his eyes still glistening. "We'll end by singing together Lacy's favorite carol, 'Joy to the World.' Lacy's family invites you to a reception in the fellowship hall following the service."

We looped through all the verses of the hymn, then filed out of the sanctuary. At our church, a parishioner's popularity can be pretty well judged by the snacks at the post-funeral reception. Several months ago, for a much-beloved elder, two ladies from the Women's League were engaged to pour

individual cups of tea into English china —
white with a smattering of delicate roses.
The women sat at each end of a long table
covered in pink damask. In between were
platters of five or six kinds of finger sandwiches, and enough cookies to add pounds
to the entire congregation — all homemade.

In Lacy's case, the pickings were slimmer
— cookies that appeared to have come out
of the Pepperidge Farm bakery rather than
someone's kitchen, a couple of paper plates
bearing triangles of white bread spread with
tuna salad, punch, and the standard urn of
decaf coffee served in heavy cardboard cups.
I wished I'd taken the time to bake something. It wasn't that folks disliked Lacy, I
thought; more that she'd been a little intimi-
dating.

I was afraid my own reception would lean
toward the grocery store cookies too. A few
close girlfriends would be genuinely grief-
stricken — Annabelle, Angie, and, yes, Janice. Assuming we'd made up by then. My
patients would miss me. But with professional situations, you never know whether
the patients are missing the real person or
the parental figure you stand for. As for the
advice column, everyone knows those au-
thors are interchangeable. I could imagine
Jillian clucking her tongue regretfully, then

moving ahead to anoint the next Dr. Aster.

I tried to shrug away the gloomy thoughts. Holidays are bad enough without a funeral layered on top. I reached for a tuna triangle, but then dropped it in the trash, thinking of Lacy's poisoned tea.

Across the room near a fake Christmas tree hung with mittens and hats, I spotted a tall, prim-looking woman with a horsey face who'd been sitting in the front pew. The spitting image of Lacy, even down to the way she crossed her arms over her chest, gripping her jacket sleeves with both hands. She looked lost. I threaded through a couple of chatting groups and went over to greet her.

"I'm Rebecca Butterman. Welcome to our church. I'm so sorry about the sad occasion of your visit."

She shook my hand firmly, then dabbed at her eyes with a lace-trimmed hankie. "I'm Lacy's younger sister, Claire. I'm grateful she had such kind people around her. We didn't get to visit too often, so it means a lot that you cared."

I stared at her a little more closely. Had she not noticed the meager snacks and the spotty turnout? I remembered my grandmother's warning on the Sunday mornings we fought about going to church.

217

"You'll need this kind of community when you grow up, Rebecca," she'd said. "When bad things happen, you'll need people who believe that human beings are basically good, most of the time. You'll want to be lifted up when things are low, and to feel many hands on you at your worst."

That was my grandmother, making the best of what people offered. I was probably too hard on my own congregation. After all, it was a weekday and not everyone could take off work at the drop of a hat, especially around the holidays. Besides, Mrs. Wiggett and Mrs. McCabe were bustling around the coffeepot, refilling cookie plates, and scurrying to fetch hot water for the odd tea drinker. And half the Women's League had attended the service. And the sexton was mopping the floor after every dripping boot. It did look like people cared.

"I'm glad it helps," I said. "We're very sorry for your loss."

"Did you know her well?" Lacy's sister cocked her head.

"Not too well," I said, "but I truly liked and admired her."

Claire ducked her head. "Reason I ask is that she seemed so happy the last few weeks. Almost like" — she cleared her throat, cheeks dimpling — "almost like she'd fallen in love." She laughed. "If you knew Lacy, you'd know what an unusual turn of events that might be. I don't think she's had a real boyfriend since her so-called romance with my cousin Dennis." She waved at the blue-suited man who had delivered part of Lacy's eulogy. "I just wondered if you had any idea who the mystery man might be?" Her eyes brimmed with tears. "I'd like to meet him," she said softly.

I shook my head, feeling like a heel. I certainly had no idea about a boyfriend. I could only think of Reverend Wesley show-ing up at her condo the Friday night she died. After eight p.m. How much did Claire know about the circumstances of her sister's murder?

"Bittersweet," I said, clasping her right hand between both of mine. "What gave you the idea there was someone special?"

"She made some comments about a younger man doing an old gal some good. I assumed it was fantasy." Claire touched her eyes with the handkerchief again.

"I'm so sorry," I murmured. "Anything we can do . . ." I was flooded with memories of my fight with Janice and guilt that we hadn't yet made up. Maybe Janice was right: Let sleeping dogs — dogs like our father — lie.

Pushing my thoughts away from my own family, I again considered the possibility that Lacy and Wesley had had a lovers' quarrel. It still didn't fit. A quarrel about something, okay. A quarrel about Paul in the pulpit, no stretch at all. A lightbulb went off: Paul was a younger man, who might well have some issues to work out regarding boundaries with his parishioners. Could Lacy have fallen in love with him?

"How long are you here for?" I asked Claire.

"Dennis and I are going back to the house to supervise the movers — they're coming tonight." Tears spilled down her cheeks.

"Could I be of some help with the sorting and packing?" I asked, thinking about the missing folder of notes, thinking I'd have a chance to paw through her drawers . . . for what?

"The movers will pack everything up," she said. "I don't have the stamina right now to go through her things. I want this over and done. I'm going to miss her so much. She and I were the only ones left. Will you excuse me, please?" She hurried off toward the bathroom.

Nice job comforting the bereaved, Rebecca. Across the room, I spotted a youngish man talking with Lacy's cousin. I trotted over.

"I think Claire could use you," I told Dennis. "She seems to be overcome." He strode off in the direction that I pointed.

I introduced myself to the handsome man in pinstripes. "Reggie Lintern," he said. "I was Lacy's boss."

"From what I hear about her work, you were lucky to have her."

"She was a dervish," Reggie agreed, "but not always a fan of playing on a team. She knew everything and she had to tell you all about it." He grimaced. "It took me a while to realize she was almost always right. How did you know her?" he asked.

"Church." I gestured to include the people in the hall. "We kind of hit it off. I write an advice column. I gather she gave a lot of advice too."

He laughed loudly. "You got that right."

"Did she seem any different to you lately?" I asked. "Any special worries or concerns?"

"Maybe a little distracted, but nothing that really stood out. Why do you ask?" He squinted.

"I feel bad about all this. And I was just wondering if there was something I could have done for her," I said. "It's always easier to see how you might have helped, looking back," I said. "Would you like a cup of coffee?"

"I need to get back to Hartford," Reggie said. "I understand the committal service is for family only." He shook my hand briskly and bolted for the door.

I approached the coffee table, scanning the crowd for Claire and wishing I'd paid closer attention to how near she was to losing it. A small white-haired woman wearing a Christmas apron was manning the drink station. "Coffee or tea?" she piped. "Oh my, I can't offer either. We seem to have run out of paper cups. How did that happen already?"

"Not to worry, I'll get them!" I said and headed for the cardboard box in the kitchen where I'd buried the Crisco. I pushed the cups aside. The can of shortening was gone. At least Meigs was doing part of his job. I carried a stack of cups back out to the coffee table, and accepted a cup of hot water from the grateful server and dunked in a Lipton tea bag that I unwrapped myself.

Mr. McCabe hurried by in the direction of his office. My mind snapped back to Lacy. Like the ministers, the sexton was always around. He might have heard the poison presentation. He might have had interactions with Lacy. He was certainly younger than she, by ten years at least.

I tried to picture the two of them together.

Not easy. He's all can-do, a practical man devoted to his work and his family. Besides, Mrs. McCabe is around a lot too — she would have surely noticed him straying and, even more surely, objected. I went back into the kitchen, tossing my cup in the trash and passing the industrial-sized ovens and the cupboards where I'd found the Crisco, to Mr. McCabe's corner office.

He sat at a desk crammed with folders, knickknacks, tools, and cleaning supplies. Mops and brooms and a shovel leaned into the corner and the walls were hung with swags of artificial greenery. A porcelain figure of a Christmas tree with two doe-eyed boys perusing the pile of presents underneath finished off the mess. The radio was on, tuned to a sports talk show. He looked up, tapping a pencil on a stack of papers, a worried smile on his lips.

"Everything okay out there?"

"Everything's good. I was just wondering whether that detective from the Guilford police department was here this morning?"

"There was a cop at the back of the church. And he did come over for a cup of coffee before the reception started. But I think he's gone already. Poor Lacy." He shook his head. "Can I help you with anything?"

"Not really. Just glad to hear they're working. Enough with the coffee breaks and donuts."

Mr. McCabe frowned fiercely. "Wait until I get my hands on the creep who pulled the grease stunt. That was just not funny."

"Not funny at all."

"How's your foot?" he asked.

"Much better."

"Put some ice on it when you get home," he warned.

"Will do, thanks. I understand the committal service is just for the family?"

He nodded. "We actually won't bury her until spring. We don't even have the ashes — the coroner only just released her. If she wants, she can sit right here waiting until the weather warms up." He grinned and waved at one of his crowded shelves. "That is, if her sister agrees. I always thought it would be awfully lonely to be waiting over at the funeral home. All those dead people . . ." He rubbed his hand over the fine stubble on his chin and sighed.

"Why not wait until spring for the service?"

"Don't get me started," he said. "Lacy's cousin came all the way from Singapore and he can't make the trip two times. He suggested putting a rush on the cremation and burying the ashes tomorrow. So I tried to dig her hole in the Memorial Garden" — he pointed to the shovel next to his desk — "but with that hard freeze, I couldn't do it. Then Lacy wasn't ready anyway, what with the autopsy and all.

"I heard she was poisoned," he added. "Who would ever think to do a thing like that?" He shook his head and reached over to grip the spade's wooden handle. "Since she's by herself, I figured I wouldn't have to go too deep, but even with my best shovel . . ." He trailed off, looking sad.

"Poor Lacy," I said.

"Hey," he said. "Did you know if it's a husband and wife they get layered one on top of the other? If you tend toward claustrophobia, let the old man go first." He chuckled grimly. "Sorry. That's a little graveyard humor."

I smiled weakly. I'd never heard him string so many words together at once. I was tempted to ask if he'd noticed anyone paying special attention to the Poison Lady, maybe even taking notes. But I'd already overstepped my bounds.

"I have a meeting. I'll see you later."

I crossed the hallway to the parlor to face the search committee — again. I was relieved to hear that Meigs had been around, though I had to admit, a little disappointed not to see him.

It suddenly occurred to me that the only person other than Paul who made frequent trips to the church basement was Mr. Mc-Cabe. Supposing he'd spread the shortening across the linoleum, he would have known perfectly well not to take those slippery stairs himself. He'd also have known where to find the Crisco and how to escape back down the stairwell and out the door on the lower level after spreading the gunk. And he seemed like the kind of man who might own a gun. And know how to use it.

But he hadn't seemed the least bit anxious during our chat — not the way I'd imagine a murderer would. And what could he possibly have against Paul? Or Lacy? Or me?

Chapter 15

In the parlor, the overhead fluorescent lights were switched on and the committee was too.

Mrs. Wiggett and Babette were seated, but Barney Brooks was pacing from one end of the room to the other. He came to a stop under the portrait of the forbidding Reverend Franklin Bower, his eyes glowing as dangerously as the oil-rendered minister's.

"I stayed awake most of the night," said Barney. "I feel I owe it to all of you and to our church to be honest about how I feel about Paul. I don't go for that men-sleeping-with-men business. Open and Affirming? Openly disgraceful, that's what I call it."

"Who said Paul was gay?" shrieked Mrs. Wiggett.

Babette was shrinking smaller and smaller into her wing chair, her expression frightened and confused.

"Just so we're all on same page," I said,

smiling at Babette, "Open and Affirming means a church welcomes people of all sexual orientations, as well as other kinds of differences. Or we would if we voted to identify our congregation that way. Which we haven't yet."

"And Lacy was not in favor of it," said Barney, "explaining quite well why she didn't support Paul's candidacy." He resumed pacing. "I remember hearing her say that if Paul comes aboard, that'll be just the impetus needed to blow our congregation into chaos. Kingdom come, I think were her exact words."

"When did she say all this to you? When?" asked Mrs. Wiggett. "I thought we were supposed to be a team."

Not a bad question. "Suppose we try to separate out the issues," I suggested in a low voice — it had worked with a psychotic patient only last month. Even though I'd stumbled home with a migraine later, I'd managed to talk him into an evaluation at the Yale ER. Barney wasn't going to be so easy.

"That will absolutely drive a wedge into our community," he insisted. "It will destroy us."

"But as Mrs. Wiggett mentioned," I said, beginning to lose my cool, "we don't know that Paul is gay. What are you basing that assumption on?" *A strong case of homophobia,* I thought to myself. *Terrified about his own unacceptable impulses.* I stood up, trying to shift the balance of power. My ankle started to ache again.

"He's overly sensitive," said Barney. "Haven't you noticed how he's always touching people?" He tightened his arms across his chest. "And he dresses too nicely."

"Ministers can't act kind and look good?" I asked. Babette nodded vigorously.

"Well, I'm sure not voting for Ellen Dark," said Mrs. Wiggett. She got to her feet too, just as Reverend Wesley opened the door and walked in. "That woman is pompous, overbearing, and entirely too sure of herself. If we have to start completely from scratch, then we'll do it."

Wesley held out his hands, a beseeching look on his face. "We're so close to wrapping this up. Would everyone please sit down?"

"He's right," I said with a grim smile. "We need to take a few steps back and practice some deep breathing. If you all feel anything like I do, it's hard to get back to work right after Lacy's funeral."

I pointed across the hall where the reception was winding down. Lacy's sister was

229

silhouetted in the entrance to the room, accepting a comforting embrace from her cousin. I glanced at Reverend Wesley. Why was he pressing the committee to forge on so soon? It didn't make sense. Why not wait until after the holidays, give everyone a chance to regroup?

"It's frightening, isn't it?" I continued. "Our friend was killed — murdered — and we don't even know who did it."

Babette bobbed her head in agreement. "Or why? Or how?"

"We know —" said Barney.

I cut him off. "Suppose we postpone our decision until after the New Year. Give the police the opportunity to do their work. We'll concentrate on a peaceful holiday and give ourselves a breather."

"I'm not in favor of that," said Reverend Wesley. He took a deep breath, pushed his shoulders down, and offered a tight smile. "Agreed. We should have waited until after the funeral."

"We can meet five years from now and I'm still not voting for a homosexual," said Barney.

Reverend Wesley's eyes bulged and he started to cough, sinking to the couch. "Paul isn't gay," he finally choked out. "Whatever gave you that idea?"

"Better a homosexual than a bossy twit!" snapped Mrs. Wiggett.

"Time out!" I said. "This meeting is adjourned. Let's meet one more time tomorrow night. I implore you all to put your personal agendas aside and think about what's best for our church. If we can't come to an agreement tomorrow, I'd suggest we go back to the council and tell them to appoint a new committee. Perhaps new blood —"

Reverend Chanton tapped on the door and beckoned to Wesley. "We're about to start the committal service for Ms. Bailes," he mouthed through the glass.

Sighing, Reverend Wesley hauled himself to his feet. "I'm sorry I lost my temper. I'm sure there won't be a need to go back to the council. Thank you all for your hard work. I appreciate your willingness to meet again tomorrow at seven. To finish this up." He padded out and fell in behind Reverend Chanton, shrugging his slumped shoulders into a black overcoat.

Barney, Babette, and Mrs. Wiggett gathered their belongings and filed out without speaking. "Thanks again," I called after them. *Thanks for what?* "See you tomorrow."

Just outside the window, I saw a small knot of Lacy's family members straggle across the parking lot and start up the hill to the memorial garden. Clouds were low in the sky and the day had turned steel gray; the limbs of the grand old hardwood trees that shaded the garden in summer hung bare and bleak. It looked like more snow was on the way. If she hadn't before this, Claire would be feeling the truth in her gut: By springtime, her older sister, reduced to ashes, would be fitted into Mr. McCabe's hole. The only thing remaining would be a small brass marker inscribed with Lacy's name.

I dialed Meigs's cell phone and was shunted to his voicemail. "It's Rebecca Butterman," I said. "The committee met. It didn't go well. Could you call me as soon as possible?"

Sinking back into the chair, I closed my eyes and tried to think. Was Lacy's death really related to the search committee? This seemed absurd. So what if Ellen was chosen over Paul or vice versa? Neither was perfect but both seemed like decent people and reasonable candidates.

Unless there was some crucial fact missing. I mulled over the balance of power in the committee. By all reports, Lacy didn't seem to like either candidate, but especially not Paul. At first, Mrs. Wiggett pushed for maturity, though she was no paragon of it herself. After today, I was certain she would only support Paul. Barney was emphatically in Ellen's camp. Babette seemed to like Paul but she was weak. She couldn't be relied on to sway anyone or even to hold her own position. Even to know exactly what her position was. Suddenly I remembered that Babette had replaced Frank Tuborg when his back went bad. And Frank was a huge fan of Paul's.

I slid open the narrow drawer in the coffee table and pulled out an old church directory. Frank and his wife grinned stiffly out of the second to last page — they lived on Opening Hill Road off Route 77. It wasn't exactly on my way, but worth a quick stop at the Big Y supermarket to pick up another token poinsettia. I'd drop by Frank's house and get his read on this mess. I was becoming expert at the faux sympathy visit.

I dialed Meigs. Again. Voicemail. Again.

"Sorry to be a bother. I know you're busy. I'm going to drop off a poinsettia at Frank Tuborg's home. I'll tell you about the committee meeting and the service when I see you. Whenever that happens to be." I pressed *end*. Damn.

Chapter 16

The Tuborgs lived in a woodsy neighborhood a half mile north of the Guilford Police Station, a mile north of Route 1. Where the path to the front door should have been, a set of small footprints had been pressed into the snow and then iced over. I tiptoed to the porch, nearly losing my footing twice, then tapped the snow off my boots and rang the bell. I seemed to have lost my manners altogether this week: Once again I was visiting with no warning and no invitation.

Frank's wife, Esther, answered, a heart-faced woman with wide hips and a warm smile. She apologized profusely for the condition of their front walk. Frank was still laid up from his surgery, she said — laid flat out on the family room divan as a matter of fact — and simply unable to attend to things the way he liked. The Women's League ladies were champions at bringing casseroles and desserts — she patted her hips — but not much on shoveling.

I passed her my anemic poinsettia. "I wonder if Frank could spare a few minutes to talk about the pastoral search committee?"

"He has nothing but time," she said and ushered me in. "He'll be so pleased about having company. And the plant."

As promised, Frank was beached on a tweed couch in front of a wide-screen TV. He gushed his thanks about the flower and pointed at a rocking chair draped in an afghan crocheted in wavelets of primary colors. "Sit yourself right down." A gas fireplace hissed, green and yellow flames flickering through the faux logs. The sweet smell of an enormous Christmas tree perfumed the air. It was trimmed with small white lights and angels made of every conceivable substance — lace, blown glass, wood, ceramic, needlepoint — even white packing foam.

"Thank goodness our son came in from Raleigh and took care of the tree," said Esther. "He strung the lights and put up the ornaments where I couldn't reach."

"It's not the one I would have chosen," Frank grumbled.

"I know, I know," said Esther, smoothing

her husband's collar. "The back is missing a branch and the top angel is crooked. No one but you notices that, dear. You didn't notice it, did you, Dr. Butterman?"

"It's gorgeous," I said, feeling heartsick at the thought of my own bare tree.

"I'll make something hot to drink." Esther bustled off to the kitchen, stopping at the TV to turn the volume down on a rerun of *Everybody Loves Raymond.*

"How are things going at the Shoreline Congregational?" asked Frank. He ran a hand through his thick white hair, flat in back from resting against the couch. Then he tucked his shirt into his corduroys, grimacing as he attempted to hoist himself up.

"Please don't try to sit up for me," I said. "Actually, things at the church are rough. For starters, we had Lacy's funeral service this morning."

He shook his head mournfully. "That's a shame. Nice lady. Why would anyone kill her? Did they find him?"

"Not that anyone's told me," I said. "And your committee" — I smiled — "is not really handling the strain very well."

Frank inched up a little on the sofa. "I'm not surprised to hear it. Miss Finster means well, but she's not going to speak up the way I would. She's no match for the others."

"Which brings me to the point of the visit," I said. "Not that I didn't want to see how you were coming along," I added hastily, my cheeks feeling suddenly warm. "Could you give me an idea of how things were shaping up before you had to withdraw?"

Esther came back into the room carrying a loaded tray: two steaming mugs of hot chocolate and a plate of Christmas cookies. She settled it on the coffee table within easy reaching distance of both Frank and me.

"The butter cookies dipped in chocolate are my favorite, but I love all of them," Frank said patting his belly. "We're starting on a new diet in January, right, Mother?" Grabbing her hand, he pulled her closer and planted a noisy smooch on her palm.

Esther giggled and swayed her hips. "No point in worrying about diets at Christmas." She leaned down to kiss his forehead and push back a hank of white hair, stuck together like a cable of undercooked spaghetti.

I pictured Esther as a guest columnist at *Bloom!* I had a feeling her advice would be very simple:

Dear Esther:
The holidays are here and I'm feel-
ing tubby and overscheduled. My
husband is complaining that I don't
have time for him. Any suggestions
for saving my sanity and the mar-
riage under these conditions?
Sincerely,
Crabby at Christmas

Dear Crabby:
Forget being chubby. Focus on
what's important: Shower your
hubby with love and homemade
cookies!

I chose a sugar cookie shaped like a pine tree frosted in green icing and dotted with tiny silver balls. "Thank you, Esther," I said. "These are works of art and I skipped lunch so I'm starving." I didn't mention that I'd avoided the funeral reception goodies for fear of being poisoned.

Grinning, she ducked her head and started back to the kitchen. Frank watched her all the way, a fond smile on his face that left me feeling a little sad.

"The committee had done fine with sur-veying the congregation and compiling the church profile," he explained. "It was just when we started to talk about actual candidates that we looked like we might run into trouble."

"Was Wesley biased from the beginning?" I asked.

Frank cocked his head, his bushy eyebrows drawing together in surprise. "I wouldn't say biased. I would say he was on a mission. Like he had a deadline — in his mind, anyway — and he was rushing us along to the finish. He wasn't ordinarily that driven about deadlines. At least, not on other committees, not in my experience."

"And Lacy?" I asked, purposefully keeping the question vague.

"Lacy didn't like being pushed," he said, reaching for a cookie, a gingerbread man iced in pink. "I guess it's okay to tell you this, now she's gone." He bit off a leg and chewed it thoughtfully, washing it down with hot chocolate. "I wondered if she was having some trouble at work. One night I asked her if everything was okay and oh boy! She was so snappish. She did let slip that she'd been under some pressure. She'd turned down the application from a big account and they'd complained. She wasn't getting a lot of support from her boss either."

"Hmm . . ." Interesting — he was the

second person to mention work stress, though her own boss hadn't told me a thing about it. "Did she mention personal troubles?" I asked. "Did you hear anything about a boyfriend?"

"Now that would be Esther's department. She gets all that kind of information from the Women's League." He winked. "Esther!" he hollered. He picked up the clicker and raised the volume on the TV. "Oh, this is funny! Ray's parents back the car through the front wall. Have you seen this one?"

I smiled politely, waiting for Esther. The smell of fried onions and something — ground beef maybe — wafted from the kitchen. Comfort food. Esther came back into the family room, wiping her hands on her apron.

"Dr. Butterman was wondering whether Lacy had a boyfriend," Frank boomed over the sitcom's squabbling family.

Esther blushed. "Frank, you didn't tell her I'm a gossip!" She leaned forward before he could deny or confirm. "We all suspected she was dating. You can always tell when a woman who's had a dry spell suddenly finds herself a man." She giggled and glanced at Frank. "Cover your ears, dear."

Frank cupped his hands over his ears, fingers spread wide, smiling.

She whispered, "We think it was Roger Kennedy."

"Roger?" Hard to picture those two together. Hard to picture anyone with Lacy, really — she'd been an imposing woman. I thought about what Roger had said at the funeral — he'd sounded like a close friend, not a lover.

"You know him," Esther insisted, perching on the couch next to her husband. "He does a lot of wedding photography on the shoreline. They say he can make any bride look beautiful, even if it's only for a day. You catch him at church every once in a while — Caryl Anderson's nephew. He lives just down the block from Lacy's place in Fetching Hill."

Frank looked puzzled.

"He took the photos at the Advent dinner," she said patiently, "all the children with Santa?" She patted Frank's stomach. "Sorry, dear — of course you weren't there this year! We hated to make Roger do it," she said to me, "especially if he and Lacy were involved and with her dying only the night before. But we didn't even know for sure they were going out. And the families count on those pictures."

"He did look glum," I agreed. At the time, I'd written it off as the nature of the photography assignment. Most of the kids forced onto Santa's lap and into holiday photos were well on their way to melting down.

Esther dropped her voice. "Mrs. McCabe said for all we knew he could have been the murderer."

I certainly hadn't gotten that kind of vibe. But between Meigs showing up at the supper, the Crisco incident, and my blind date with Bob, I hadn't paid much attention to anyone else. I winced. I *still* hadn't called Bob back. Then it struck me that Roger's station just outside the church hall adjacent to the restrooms was close to the stairwell where Paul and I had fallen. Had the police thought to question him about whom he might have seen? Would he have had time between photographic disasters to frost the stairs with Crisco? I added him to my mental list.

"Isn't that sad?" Esther asked. "Here Lacy found a man to ring her chimes and she didn't live long enough to really enjoy him." She clucked her tongue and patted Frank again. "Sure you won't stay for supper? I'm making stuffed peppers — my mother-in-law's recipe. The secret is extra onions and sausage instead of ground beef."

My mouth watered but my muscles ached, my nose had started to run again, and a dull pain was edging back into my sinuses. I wanted to pop aspirin and decongestants and crawl into bed, but first I wanted to talk to Curt one more time and insist he tell the police everything he'd seen Friday night.

I thanked Frank and Esther, accepted a tinfoil packet of cookies for the road, and drove north to Fetching Hill. I parked in the lot by the tennis courts, pulled on my hat and gloves, and started up the hill toward Curt and Sharon's condo. A green Subaru pulled into the driveway right in front of me. Roger Kennedy got out. I froze, my heart pounding like a trapped bunny.

"Good afternoon," he said pleasantly, as he exited from his vehicle.

"Hi." I made the split-second decision to talk with him briefly — at the first sign of menace, I'd run like the wind, yelling for Curt. "Aren't you Roger Kennedy?"

He looked surprised, but not worried or angry.

"I heard you speak at Lacy's service. That was lovely," I said. "I'm a friend of hers from church." He closed his car door and came over to greet me.

"You were in AA together, right? Friends of Bill?"

He nodded and grinned. "You too?"

"No, I write an advice column. So Lacy and I had a lot in common — the urge to help people — too much sometimes."

"Absolutely true," he said. "You have to be careful about offering support without getting overinvolved, no matter how long you've been sober." He adjusted his wire-rimmed glasses, which had slid a half inch down his nose. "We lost a good friend." A muscular striped cat with a tan bull's-eye on his flank trotted out from behind the garage and wound through Roger's legs. "You old bear," he said, scooping him up and rubbing his chin on the fur between the cat's ears.

This man had not killed Lacy, I'd risk my clinical reputation on that. "I'm going out on a limb here and guess you were her sponsor?"

"No harm in telling you you're right," he said. "And I'm sick about what happened to her. If only I'd listened harder . . ."

"Listened to what?"

He placed the big cat down on the pavement. "I called her Friday night. She couldn't talk because someone had stopped in."

I tried not to look as alarmed as I felt. "Friday night? Any idea about who?"

"She was worried about their drinking,

245

that's all I know." He shook his head mournfully. "You see, if only I'd asked. But I was too busy telling her to mind her own affairs because this person wasn't going to accept her help until he was good and damn ready." He pulled his glasses off and wiped his sleeve across his eyes. "If only I'd dropped in to check on her . . ."

"You can drive yourself mad with that sort of thinking," I said kindly. "You told the cops?"

He nodded. "Knowing Lacy, she kept notes on everything. I'm sure they'll find them."

"One more thing," I said. "Saturday night at the church supper, did you see anyone go down the stairs before Paul Cashman fell?"

"Sorry, no. I was protecting my equipment from little hooligans." He grinned.

We shook hands, Roger promising to keep in touch. Why did I care so much about this woman, anyway?

You don't, said a scolding voice inside my head that sounded suspiciously like Dr. Goldman. *You're a lonely divorcée with a crush on a married man. Whose wife is deathly ill.*

I pushed those thoughts away. Lacy deserved my attention. I hoped someone would do the same for me if I expired suddenly. End of story.

I trudged up the hill toward Curt's condo. There was no leftover snow and ice on this sidewalk — either Curt or Sharon had scraped the pavement dry. I rang the doorbell, slapping my upper arms and marching in place to keep warm. A heavy gray shelf of clouds had dropped to the horizon and the air felt damp and cold. More snow was on the way.

A woman answered my knock after a long pause. She was dressed in flannel pajamas covered with cats playing harps and a ratty green robe that looked like it could have wrapped around her twice. Her hair was pulled back into a lank ponytail and her nose was red and swollen.

"I'm sorry," I said. "You must be Sharon. I'm Rebecca Butterman — I met Curt the other day. I sure hope I didn't wake you."

She moved aside and waved me in. "I've come down with a cold, that's all. Don't you hate that? Curt told me all about you." She closed the door behind us.

I nodded, hoping I hadn't passed him the germs, then on to her. Also hoping he hadn't mentioned the illicit tour of Lacy's place. "I was hoping to speak to Curt."

"He's bowling today," she said, cracking a grin. "Nothing keeps him from the lanes —

not even a bad back and workers' compensation. Thank the dear Lord, it's a little challenging to have that big lug home all the time."

I smiled back. "Curt mentioned that Lacy had visitors on Friday. Before she died. I got to thinking he might remember more about them than what he'd told me at first."

She nodded, then blew her nose into a supersized hankie. "We wondered about that. She had a busy evening — unusual for Lacy." She stuffed the handkerchief back in the pocket of her robe. "I'm going to say she had three different visitors."

"I'm hoping that he told the police about all this," I said sternly.

Sharon looked embarrassed. "You have to understand my husband," she said. "He won't even let me get a discount card at the supermarket, never mind talk directly to the cops. He doesn't want a record of anything on the books — even groceries. Big Daddy is always watching." She sneezed three times in quick succession.

"Bless you," I said. "But isn't it a bit unsettling to have the killer on the loose, when you live right next door to the victim?" I knew exactly how that felt — both Babette Finster and I had lived through it last September.

Sharon nodded again, then began to look more worried. "I guess I was assuming it was someone she knew. That it wouldn't have anything to do with us." She waved me into the living room. "That poor lady didn't deserve to die, even if she was a little unfriendly."

"How about if I tell the cops to come up and interview you and Curt themselves?"

"You don't understand. Curt will tell them something flat-out wrong, just on principle. We can't help it." She shrugged. "It's just the kind of folks we are."

Flat-out crazy, I thought.

"The cops were here again earlier today," Sharon said. "They were inside her place for a while, looking for something I guess. Clues?" She glanced over, seeming to notice that I was starting to sweat. "Have a seat," she said. "Take off your coat. How about a snack?"

"Thank you, but I can't stay." I perched on the edge of a faded paisley couch and unbuttoned my coat's top buttons. I wasn't looking for another tea and cookies visit, just get the information and get the heck out. Still I knew I'd have to admire the tree. Sharon had positioned me directly in front of it, even bigger and busier than the Tuborgs', and underneath, an extravaganza of wrapped presents. "Beautiful tree," I said.

Sharon beamed and sat down next to me, pulling the robe's belt tight around her belly. "My Curt's nothing but a big kid. Even with our girls living in California, he wouldn't dream of cutting back."

"Tell me what you noticed on Friday night." If there was no other way, I'd get what details I could and then confess everything to Meigs.

"The last fellow to visit was her minister — you probably know that. He's the one who called the cops. It was late for Lacy — I'm going to say close to nine when he came. Curt doesn't sleep much, so he entertains himself by patrolling the neighborhood. He's harmless," she added apologetically.

"As far as you know then, Reverend Wesley called the police right away?"

Sharon nodded. "Couldn't have been more than ten or fifteen minutes after he got there."

"Who else?" I asked, thinking she must not sleep much either.

"The others we didn't recognize. One came right after dark. A slender man in a dark coat."

"A boyfriend?" I wondered.

"Oh no, that wasn't Roger. He lives just

down the end of the drive and he'd never take a car up to see her. He's one of those tree huggers, always thinks catastrophe's around the corner so better hoard your resources and walk as much as you can. Good Lord, this is a man who'd bicycle to the Big Y and then strap his groceries on the rack and pedal home."

"In the winter?" I asked.

She smiled. "Well, maybe not in a blizzard. We couldn't see how they had all that much in common. Except maybe feeling lonely. Must be hard to be single, taking all those wedding pictures."

I felt fairly confident that Roger hadn't been her boyfriend, but what difference did it make now? "So it wasn't Roger," I prompted. "But you're sure it was a man?"

She nodded vigorously. "Then just after supper came a woman. Stubby, I think Curt would say. She stayed a little longer."

"How old?" I asked. This might have been the person Lacy was talking with when Roger called her. It might have been the killer.

"Not that we saw her up close," said Sharon, a little defensive now, "but I wouldn't say too young. On the short side — maybe about your height. And maybe a little heavy. Though it's hard to tell with everyone wearing those puffy winter coats, isn't it? I guess they keep you warm but they don't have much style." She started to cough. "You feel free to come back later and talk to Curt. He'll be home after five. I just hate not being hospitable but I've got to go to bed."

I could see that she meant it. No false politeness here.

"You take care," I said. "I'll let myself out."

I minced down the steps and paused on the sidewalk to study Lacy's condo. From Sharon's descriptions, it almost sounded as if the two ministerial candidates visited. And then our minister. But why? Why would she interview them alone? This was totally against the search committee guidelines.

And would this mean that one of them came bearing poison?

Chapter 17

It began to sleet. I pulled my scarf up over my head. Time to call Meigs and tell all. I punched in the number of his cell phone. Big surprise, shunted to voicemail. "It's Rebecca Butterman. Please call when you get a chance."

Starting down the street, I could just make out the lines of Lacy's back deck, including the beam that housed her spare key. Claire and her movers would be arriving shortly to pack up the condo and carry every loose thread of Lacy's life across the country. The moment was now — or never.

Hugging the aluminum siding, I ducked into the shadows, stripped off my right glove, and felt along the underside of the deck until the key jingled against the nail. I took it down, inserted it into the lock, and slid the door open. Once inside, I eased off my boots and left them on the same mat Curt and I had used the day before.

With a deep breath, I glanced at my watch and started up the stairs, giving myself five minutes to look around and get the hell out.

The door at the top of the basement stairs opened onto a small hallway that fed into the kitchen on the right and the dining room/living room on the left. The condo was dim and quiet and very cold. Should I inch up the heat for Lacy's sister? It would be bad enough to arrive under these sad circumstances without freezing to death in the process. But then she'd wonder who'd messed with the thermostat. *Keep your damn focus, Rebecca.* I glanced at my watch. Four minutes left.

With a noisy grind and clatter, the refrigerator's ice maker sprang to life, causing my pulse to race. Lacy's note was still pinned to the white metal door:

Polish the silver today if you have the time. LB.

Who was Lacy's cleaning lady? Sharon would probably know. This could be important because the hired help often see more than anyone means them to. I made a mental note to call Sharon back, another day when it wasn't dark and cold and she wasn't sick and I wasn't so damn scared that I imagined everyone was a murderer. Or better still, just mention it to Meigs — if he ever called me. Thirty more seconds had ticked by.

I turned slowly around the room, looking for anything out of place. The dishwasher was cracked open, the row of red lights I'd seen with Curt now off. There were no dishes in the drainer. How had the killer administered the poison? I pulled my glove back on and tugged open the washer door. Two white china dinner plates edged in swirls of ivy leaves were nestled in the bottom, nothing up above. Maybe the cops had found something and carried it off.

I skated down the hall in my stocking feet, sliding over the polished oak floor, and started up the stairs. At the top, I turned left into Lacy's office. I couldn't see well with only the faint light from a street lamp filtering into the room. I switched on a small desk lamp, pulled open the top desk drawer, and felt around at the back. My fingers closed over a set of small keys. Breathing shallowly, I fitted the key into the top drawer of the file cabinet and slid it open.

I thumbed through the files, all labeled in Lacy's round script: paid bills, taxes, health insurance, activities pending. Activities pending? I opened the folder. Lacy had made reservations for a trip to Duluth in May. And she had season tickets to a chamber music series at Yale this winter. And one ticket to *La Traviata* at the Metropolitan Opera in March. Sad that she would go alone. Actually, no. Brave that she'd go alone, sad that she wouldn't be going at all.

I tucked the folder back in the drawer and riffled through the remaining files. At the back was one labeled "Shoreline Congregational Church Search." "Confidential" was written on the outside in neat block letters. I pulled it out of the drawer — the folder was empty. Probably the cops already had its contents. My heart pounded and I felt nauseous. Time to get out. Go by the police station. Tell Meigs my thoughts, meet with the committee tomorrow night, do the best I could to moderate a decision. Resign.

I turned off the light and crept back down the stairs; I'd crossed over more than a self-imposed time line. Breaking and entering, stealing, lying, I'd done it all. Why couldn't I trust Meigs to run a professional investigation? Would I ever learn to trust that a man would take care of me?

The same streetlight that had shone onto Lacy's desk reflected off the collection of Hummels in the living room. I hadn't noticed Lacy's miniature Christmas tree, which sat on the coffee table — a fake fir that looked like it had been unfolded from a box in the attic. I was definitely going to do something about my own tree tomorrow. Suddenly a beam of light blinded me.

"Stop right where you are and put your hands on your head," boomed a stern voice.

I raised my arms, heart now beating like a terrified bird, then covered my eyes with one hand against the light. "It's Rebecca Butterman. A friend of Lacy's?" I wouldn't have believed it either.

"I found the switch," said another deep male voice and the fluorescent kitchen light flooded the scene. Two Guilford policemen had their guns trained on me.

CHAPTER 18

On the short ride to the police station in the back of the cruiser, I focused on exactly how I'd explain all this to Meigs. Or if he wasn't there, the cop in charge of the shift. Which would be worse? Eeny, meeny, miny, moe . . .

At least the question kept me from wallowing in the deep humiliation of having been frisked and then trotted out Lacy's front door with my arm twisted behind my back, watched by the shocked and puzzled faces of Lacy's sister, her cousin, the movers, and the neighbors, including both Curt and Sharon. Who now had more ammunition for their anti-cop sentiments.

"Dr. Butterman?" Claire had asked tremulously. I just waggled the fingers of my free hand, face burning.

The scanner buzzed and chattered as the two cops discussed where to pick up dinner. They seemed to be settling on Nick's

Place, a popular greasy spoon in a strip mall just over the Madison line. Officer Kent, with a red face and thinning gray hair, was picturing split pea soup and a cheeseburger. Potbellied Officer Scott wanted pot roast and mashed potatoes. I chose not to remind them Nick's wasn't open on Sunday night. My own stomach churned with the remnants of Esther Tuborg's cookies — my anxiety rendering them a total waste of calories.

Officer Kent pulled the cruiser around the back of the station and nosed into the garage. Officer Scott swung out of the passenger seat and opened my door. He wasn't smiling. He'd been the one to retrieve my boots from the basement and return Lacy's key to the beam: In his eyes, the cold look told me, I was at best a sneak and at worst a criminal.

"Let's go, Doctor," he said.

I trailed him into the back hallway where he stashed his gun in a safe on the wall and spun the combination lock. We were buzzed into the jail. From a distance, the cells didn't look too bad — suburban bare and reasonably clean. But being locked up would make the shame complete. Would this show up in the police blotter? Would my patients see it?

"Have a seat," Officer Scott said, gesturing to a gray plastic chair in front of the fingerprint station. "Detective Meigs is on his way."

I slumped into the plastic chair. A blurry, fun-house version of my face reflected off the glass of the computer screen. My hair had frizzed into a wild bird's nest — seagull or osprey, maybe — and my nose appeared swollen to twice its normal size. I smoothed down the worst of the hair, practiced a conciliatory smile, and decided a regretful frown might have a better effect. I startled at the sound of voices.

"She's in the back," said Officer Scott from down the hall. "She wasn't carrying a weapon. We made sure of that," he said as they came into view. He smirked at Meigs. "We were going to arrest her for criminal trespass, but she insisted you'd asked her to look into some things."

Meigs just glared, first at him and then at me.

"I'll take it from here," he said and gestured to me without meeting my gaze. "Follow me." He strode down the hallway, turning the corner into an interview room, then pointing to the chair on one side of a gray metal desk. I sat, laced my hands together, and brought them to my forehead.

"I'm sorry —"

"We're past sorry." Meigs held both palms up and began pacing the short length of the room. Three steps across, three steps back. He looked haggard and furious, beyond furious, really. And I couldn't blame him. I'd stepped way over the line and been stupid enough to get caught, completely embarrassing him in the process.

He slapped the desk and sat down, pressing his fingers to his temples.

"I'd like to know how you progressed from attending a church meeting to breaking into a murdered woman's home. What was the thinking on that?"

"You didn't call back" — Meigs dropped his head onto his fists — "and there were a couple of leads that came up."

His head jerked back up. His hands were shaking and he glowered so fiercely I wondered if his eyes would pop out; he'd like to wring someone's neck. "I distinctly recall saying you were not on the case. I'm quite sure I said it more than once. Do you have some kind of a death wish?"

"I'm sorry. It was a mistake to go into Lacy's house. I admit that and I'm sorry. But —"

"No buts," he shouted. "You're a civilian, a psychologist, not a detective. Do you not understand what you did was against the law? And you did this believing that someone shot at you last night. Are you some kind of idiot?"

"Excuse me," I said, getting to my feet. My coat caught on the back of the chair and I yanked it free. "Are we finished here?"

"No, we are not finished," he said. "Sit the fuck down."

I sat, first frightened and then fuming. I reminded myself that I hadn't just "stopped by" — the cops had picked me up after I'd broken into someone's home. Officer Kent had explained that fact rather thoroughly.

Meigs rubbed his eyes and then pinched the bridge of his nose with his fingers. "I'm sorry," he grunted. "I shouldn't have called you an idiot."

"Even if I act that way?" I asked.

He allowed a tired smile. "You're killing me," he said, jerking a thumb over his shoulder. "These guys are merciless when they see a soft spot. But the main thing is you put yourself in jeopardy. And for what reason? That's what I don't get. What is the matter with you?"

What *was* the matter? I felt frightened and stupid. This wasn't the first time I'd put myself in danger for a single dead woman. This time, it all boiled down to impressing

Meigs. Sort of. The hazy feelings burbling a little deeper promised to be completely embarrassing. When in doubt, change the subject.

"How did your officers know I was in Lacy's house?"

"You turned the light on in the front room around the time her sister arrived."

"I am an idiot." I smiled. "I'd make a lousy burglar. And not much of a cop."

"Let's hear about your 'detective' work."

I forced myself to ignore the audible quote marks in his voice — tonight I deserved whatever he dished out.

"I remembered that Babette Finster had replaced Frank Tuborg on the committee. Seemed like it would be worth getting his impressions."

"Go on," he said curtly.

I told him about the visit to Esther and Frank Tuborg's house, their comments about Lacy having a new boyfriend and possible trouble at work. "I don't think she had a new boyfriend — I think she was content with herself and people misconstrued that. You can be single and be happy."

"Is that so?" he said.

"Roger Kennedy said he told you about calling Lacy the night she died?"

Meigs nodded.

I paused. "This wasn't the first time I'd been in Lacy's home."

The grim set of his mouth got grimmer.

"When I went up on Sunday to look around, I met one of her neighbors, Curt Fisher. He said he knew where her key was and that he had permission to use it."

"Permission from who? The woman was dead, goddammit. We're in the middle of a goddamn murder investigation." He ground his teeth and swallowed, then began to massage his forehead in little circles. "This case gets screwed up by you and this buffoon of a neighbor and I'll be directing pedestrian traffic in a school zone."

"I'm sorry," I said, my voice sounding shaky and meek. "Maybe it's this head cold. Maybe I wasn't thinking clearly, but when Mr. Fisher offered, I just went. Do you want to hear the rest or not?"

"Go on," he croaked. "Do I need this?" he muttered to himself as he pulled a notepad out of his inside jacket pocket.

"You hung up on me last time we talked," I said. "I thought I overheard someone saying you were headed to Fetching Hill. So I drove up to meet you, thinking we could talk and maybe you'd want to look for Lacy's notes. I sensed that she was guarding some kind of secret from the rest of the committee."

He rolled his eyes. This was quite a story. And the good parts were still to come.

"Curt's an old hippie," I explained. "He saw people visit Lacy Friday night but no way in hell was he going to call you guys."

Meigs scowled and made a note on his pad. "Great. That's just swell."

"He doesn't like cops. I'm not the only one who doesn't find macho shows of force endearing," I said defiantly. "Once I told him my problem, he offered to show me around. But I wouldn't allow him to hack into the file cabinets."

"So you do have limits," said Meigs. "Or you did a couple days ago."

I glared. "Paul Cashman's hiding something. I don't know if it's about Wesley or himself. Barney Brooks thinks he's gay but I don't agree."

"And that would relate to what?"

I heaved a sigh. "The search for a minister, of course. Isn't that what you asked me to help with? And by the way, you should follow up on the Friday night visitors. Sharon said there were three, not just two."

He looked amazed. "You think we're total morons."

"Could I possibly have a drink of water? I've got a splitting headache."

Meigs lumbered into the hallway. I dug a little bottle of aspirin out of my purse and rested my head on the desk, closing my eyes. What *was* the matter with me? My cell phone vibrated. I fished it out from my rear pants pocket. Angie's name flashed on the screen. Before I could answer, Meigs returned with a paper cone filled with water. I swallowed two aspirin.

"Is there more?" he asked.

"Roger said she made notes on everything she did. Even Wesley saw some in the typing queue." I hurried on before he could interrupt. "That's why I went into her condo today. That's why I had to get into the file cabinet. But the contents of the folder were gone. We need to find that stuff."

He stared at me until I blushed.

"I mean . . . maybe you need to look for that stuff."

Meigs shook his head as if to clear his brains of static. "Your reasoning eludes me."

"I'm sorry," I said again. "And you might want to check on who cleaned her house." I started to sniffle.

Meigs's frown softened and he patted the table in front of my hands. "We're on it, really. We found sprigs of lily of the valley in a vase in her kitchen greenhouse. We think the poisoned water was added to her tea."

I hadn't even thought to look at the greenhouse — too busy poking in the half-empty dishwasher.

"Did you find fingerprints on the Crisco?" I snuffled and pulled a Kleenex from my purse.

"The Crisco?" he asked, shoulders stiffening.

"I left you a text message about that too," I said. "And a voicemail." I blew my nose and dabbed at my eyes. "The can of lard I hid in the coffee cups: Were there prints on it?"

"I don't know what you're talking about," he said.

"But you came by to pick up the can after I called," I said.

He shook his head.

"Damn," I said. "Then who has it?"

CHAPTER 19

"Start at the beginning," said Meigs. He was trying to hide his worry, but the tough cop act was fading.

"While I was waiting for the committee meeting on Sunday, I poked through the cupboards in the church kitchen, just to see if we had Crisco."

Meigs sighed, started to say something, but then sighed again and motioned for me to continue.

"I found two cans. One full, one with what looked like finger marks in it — as though someone had reached in and scooped out a handful. I was late for the meeting so I hid that can, thinking you'd pick it up later."

"I didn't get that message," he said. "When did you send it?"

"It must have been Sunday." I thought back over the last few days. "Yes, Sunday. Because I came to coffee hour a little early and no one else was around. The first one was a text — I'm not too good at those. So who has the can?" I repeated.

Meigs got to his feet. "I'll send someone over tomorrow to look around. Meanwhile, do I need to spell this out?" His gaze bored into me. "You're O-F-F the case."

"You said that." I stood up too. "I have to attend tomorrow's committee meeting. I can't bail on them now. I promise I won't try to solve anything besides the mystery of why five people can't agree on a minister."

"Fine," he said. "I'll go with you."

I shook my head and scowled. "No one's going to talk freely with you there."

He blew out a big sigh. "Go to the meeting, talk to the people, and then drive straight home. I'm going to post an officer near the church. Once you're back in your own living room with the front door locked, call me." He made a slashing motion across his neck. "Then you're done. *Finito.* Let's go. I'll run you up to your car."

I followed him out through the back of the station, the same way I'd come in. I felt floppy and weak, like a sack of flour losing its contents through a hole punched in the bottom. Meigs nodded at the two cops who'd brought me in an hour earlier. They kept their faces expressionless as I passed by.

The air outside was damp and freezing cold and the light had already leeched from the sky. Was this the shortest day of the year? It certainly hadn't felt that way. Meigs unlocked and flung open the passenger side door of his van, then strode to the driver's side without helping me in. Fine. That's the way I wanted it. He hummed on the way to Fetching Hill. "Joy to the World" it might have been, if he could have carried a tune.

He pulled to a stop in front of the tennis court parking lot, engine idling. While I started my car, he hopped out and scraped a layer of ice and snow off my windows. I rolled my window down.

"Thanks. For all your help." I bit my lip and smiled sheepishly. "Please tell me I'm not going to end up in the police blotter."

"You should have thought of that before you broke into Ms. Bailes's home. Do we need to post a guard to keep you out of trouble?"

"I'll be fine."

"Be careful," he said. "Just go home. Lock your doors and set the damn alarm."

I rolled the window back up, locked the car doors, and waved as he drove off. The lights were blazing in Lacy's condo just up the road. Should I knock and try to explain? I pictured the scene inside the house: boxes open, Hummel figurines half packed, Claire weeping as she directed the movers sorting through the detritus of her sister's life. What if I arrived just as she found the springtime ticket to Duluth? Once again, what was I supposed to say?

I dialed Angie instead.

"Any chance you could pick up some Chinese food and meet me at my house?"

"Excellent," she said. "What do you want?"

"Won ton soup, scallion pancakes, General Tso's chicken, vegetable fried rice. And sesame noodles. And an order of fried dumplings with extra sauce."

Angie laughed. "You're not pregnant, are you?"

" 'Tis the season for immaculate conception." I hung up and started home.

The little white cardboard boxes were spread across the coffee table, the air saturated with the smell of garlic and ginger and wood smoke. Inspired by Frank and Esther, I'd built a small fire with my fake logs courtesy of Stop and Shop supermarket. As we ate, Angie scolded me for not returning Bob's call, breaking into Lacy's condo, and carrying a hopeless torch for Meigs. I speared the last dumpling with my chopsticks and dipped it into the pungent sauce.

"Meigs isn't worried about the missing Crisco can?" she asked.

"I think he's more worried than he showed me. But really, the two incidents are not very similar. What do poisoned tea and Crisco have in common?"

"The kitchen?" said Angie. She pushed Spencer away from her plate. "Don't even think about it, cat. The killer knows his way around the kitchen."

"Not necessarily," I said. "You can wield a tea bag and a can of lard without knowing how to cook. Who had the motive both to kill Lacy and ambush Paul?"

"I can't see how they'd be connected," Angie said. She scraped a second helping of fried rice onto her plate and covered it with chicken in spicy sauce.

I shrugged. "Other than the search committee antics — and I've gotten nowhere with that." I bit into the dumpling. "I did read an interesting interview with P. D. James the other night."

Angie looked puzzled.

"She's a famous British mystery writer."

"Your detective's gonna love this one — solve his crime using someone's fiction."

"Find wisdom wherever you can," I said.

272

"Believe me, it isn't coming from Meigs's cops. Anyway. James had a great line for her detective. Something about how all the motives for murder start with the letter L: love, lust, lucre, and loathing. And that love is the most dangerous of all."

"I'll buy it in theory," Angie said. "Let's imagine Paul and Lacy were involved." She tapped her teeth with her chopsticks. "They were having a passionate love affair and then she realized — suddenly — that he was too young for her. And that it was inappropriate to be having sex with an intern. Not that this would stop a politician, mind you, but she remembers she's representing the church. So she ends the affair, but Paul's devastated. He rushes up to her apartment to beg her to reconsider, and when she holds steady, he serves her the poisoned tea, which he's handily prepared ahead of time just in case the conversation doesn't go the way he wanted."

I giggled helplessly. "P. D. James has nothing on you."

"When he realizes what he's done and that there will be most serious consequences" — she drew her eyebrows together — "he spreads the Crisco across the stairs and falls down in order to divert suspicion."

Gasping with laughter, I wiped my eyes

and blew my nose.

She smiled. "At least I got you laughing. I could spin the same kind of tale with Reverend Wesley and your new friend Roger, but I have to get home." She picked up our plates and carried them to the kitchen while I gathered the leftovers. Depositing the plates on the counter, she turned to offer a hug. "You'll stay out of trouble? And call poor sweet Bob?"

I nodded. Once Angie left, I filled the bathtub with hot, hot water and an herbal bath salt mix called Ancient Secrets. Sliding into the fragrant and steaming tub, I felt my muscles relax a little. Spencer hopped up onto the edge, patted the water gingerly, then licked his paw.

The P. D. James line I'd been trying to remember for Angie crystallized and I quoted it for the cat. "They'll tell you, laddie, that the most dangerous emotion is hatred. Don't believe them. The most dangerous emotion is love." Spencer walked away.

I drained the water, patted my shriveled skin dry, and got into my nightgown, feeling restless. I sorted through my E-mail — nothing but spam.

Then I opened the Dr. Aster folder and dashed off a column on the Women's

League question — how to gracefully reduce the size of your Christmas card list. I considered getting a jumpstart on January: Time and advice columns wait for nobody. Couldn't make myself do it. On a day like today, it was hard to believe anyone would — or should — listen to me. Not about real problems.

That was the trouble with the gig: It started to seep into my consciousness, making me feel as though I really did have answers. Whereas my actions this afternoon showed that my judgment was just as lousy as the desperate women who wrote Dr. Aster — pining after married men, making boneheaded choices, and sticking their fat heads into problems that weren't their business.

Chapter 20

I woke early the next morning and tried to visualize which patients would be drifting, moaning, marching through my day. The next thought floated up like a helium balloon. Wednesday: my day off. Too late to get back to sleep — the events of the last half week crowded in, whirling through my brain like tumbleweeds. It might have been easier to go to the office and focus on other people's problems.

I extracted my leg from under the covers and rotated the ankle: hardly sore. The swelling had gone down and the purple color was shifting to sallow. I continued the self-assessment: My sniffles lingered but just barely. A case of acute embarrassment about my trip to the police station lingered too.

And questions still buzzed my brain like flies on a corpse. Meigs had banned me from further outings, but maybe I could use my psychological expertise — for once. Who at the church was acting strange? Reverend Wesley, I had to admit. The picture of Beverly Sandifer came to mind. Could the end of their marriage be related to this mess?

Spencer hopped up onto the bed and butted my hand with his head, purring loudly. "Did you start the coffee?" I asked.

I rolled out of bed, wrapped up in Mark's old robe, and headed into the kitchen, clutching the laptop. While the coffee brewed and the cat ate breakfast, I booted up the computer and opened my E-mail, deleting a list of spam and then clicking on a message from Annabelle.

R: This is totally against my better judgment but . . . I ran into a friend from the divinity school who happens to know your young man rather well. Don't even ask me the name; this is strictly background material. Anyway, this unnamed person just happened to reveal that your young man, nameless, had consulted with her on a serious matter at the church where he was interning. Somehow I got the idea it was a harassment case. I can't be sure, I'm trying to read between the lines.

Anywho, she encouraged him to take

it up with the parties involved before filing any kind of formal complaint. That's all I know. I know no more. Hope it helps. You can't use it to ask questions because it didn't come from me, but maybe you can listen for it. You are a trained professional! Good luck with your committee. Call me about lunch. XO, Annabelle

The computer chimed with a message from Janice labeled "Brittany's tea." I poured a cup of coffee and braced myself to open it. The tone of the message was icy:

Have you forgotten about taking Brittany to Christmas tea?

I was going to have to tackle her head on. Soon. My life was complicated enough without suffering the cold shoulder from my own sister over the holidays.

"Wouldn't miss it for the world," I wrote back, though in truth it had slipped my mind. "I'll pick her up at four."

As part of my annual Christmas gift to my niece, I plan a special outing for the two of us. This year, with Brittany in her Barbie/fairy-princess phase, we "girls" had a reservation at the tea shop in Madison. I wasn't exactly in the mood for acting out holiday cheer, but the promise was important. And I knew I'd feel better after. Brittany has that effect.

I cut up a handful of strawberries, added blueberries picked and frozen last summer, and whirled them with yogurt and honey into a smoothie. I sipped this alongside a double serving of cinnamon toast and more coffee, all the while puzzling over the meaning of Annabelle's tip.

Had Paul been harassed by Reverend Wesley? Then why would Wesley be Paul's ferocious fan? Blackmail? *Wesley?* I shook my head. And Wesley wouldn't tell me a damn thing even if I pressed him — he hadn't so far. I decided to phone our former assistant, the Reverend Leo Sweeney, a second time. He had nothing to lose — he no longer worked at our church. I shuffled through the papers in my briefcase and found the New Hampshire number.

"Might I speak with assistant pastor Reverend Sweeney?" I asked the sprightly voice on the other end of the line. Not the same woman who'd answered earlier this week.

"Reverend Sweeney?" she wondered, sounding puzzled. Or clueless. "Assistant pastor?"

"Yes, Reverend Sweeney," I said. "Leo

Sweeney?"

"Oh, you mean our Sunday school super-intendent!" she said with enthusiastic relief. "Leo's not in yet but I can put you through to his voicemail. He said he'd be in his office all day."

"Sunday school superintendent?" I repeated. "That's okay. I'll call back."

I hung up abruptly. Sunday school? How could that be? No way Leo would have taken a position so much below his education and experience — unless he'd gone out under a dark cloud. He'd be unlikely to tell me the truth about this over the phone. I pulled on a pair of brown corduroys and a yellow turtleneck, then added my favorite chunky necklace, Uggs, and a camel-hair blazer. With any luck, I could zip up to the New Hampshire border, get the facts from Leo, and be back in Madison in plenty of time to take Brittany to tea.

With the traffic gods beaming down on me, I whipped through the tail end of the Hartford rush hour in no time flat. The NPR news predicted more violence in the Middle East and a winter storm watch for the shoreline. I switched to a classical music station with no news of any kind and set the cruise control to seventy-two. Even a mean cop looking for trouble wouldn't bother with a Honda going seven miles over the speed limit.

As the middle of Massachusetts flashed by, frozen and snowy, I puzzled over the mysteries of Reverend Leo. What was the deal with Ellen Dark? He hadn't been particularly complimentary or enthusiastic about her. And why had he really left our church?

I tried to refresh the details of our last conversation. One new fact made its way to the surface: Leo had said his wife was busy with the twins — and a job. I'd been too busy nosing into Wesley and Beverly's story to allow that to sink in. Wasn't it odd to take a job with new twin babies in the house? Not that I wanted to judge. There are plenty of theories about what kind of mother produces the best kind of child — most of them designed to make the women feel guilty about how much they're juggling. In the end, it's individual. Daria Sweeney might have appeared to be a matronly homebody, but when the physical and emotional reality of two squalling infants confronted her, work outside the home might be what kept her sane.

I found the Barstow church just three miles off the highway, knocked the snow from my boots, and asked the dizzy receptionist for directions to Leo's office.

"Down the stairs to the right and follow the mural to the end of the hall. He's right next to the fishes and loaves." She giggled.

Through the half-glass door, I could see Leo hunched over the computer. His office, small to begin with, was crammed with the trappings of Sunday school — toys, books, children's hymnals, stacks of fill-in-the-blanks and color-in-the-lines work sheets and a giant replica of Noah's Ark, complete with pairs of faded plush animals. I tapped on the window and stepped inside without waiting for an invitation.

"Can I help . . ." His cheery expression fell away as soon as he recognized me. "Dr. Butterman!" he sputtered as he got to his feet. "What a pleasant surprise."

Clearly it wasn't. "Sorry to drop in without calling ahead." I wasn't. "There are a few questions I didn't feel I could ask over the phone." I stared until he lowered his eyes and pointed to a chair.

I rolled a doll-baby carriage aside, moved a stuffed elephant to the floor, and sat down. "Forgive me for being blunt, but why did you leave your position at our church in such a hurry? To take a job as superintendent of this Sunday school," I added, to be sure he knew I meant business.

He sank into his chair, rolled his head back, and then swung it forward and fixed his gaze on me. "I'm assuming you will keep this conversation between us?"

I folded my arms across my chest and frowned. Leo heaved a sigh.

"This will sound awful." He tilted his head, brows raised, and grimaced. "But maybe, being a psychologist, you'll be able to appreciate how flawed we humans can be."

I gave him a blank look.

"Daria and I were not getting along. She hated being so far from her family. She felt she couldn't make any true friends of her own, being the minister's wife. She was miserable and she was making my life miserable too." He ran a hand through his blond curls. "Just as I was coming to the conclusion that we weren't meant to be together, that she couldn't fully understand or support the commitment I'd made to serving God, she turned up accidentally pregnant."

"Accidentally?" I asked. *Commitment?* I thought.

"You know what I mean," he said. "It wasn't planned." He worked his frown into a smile. "God works in mysterious ways."

"You left Shoreline Congregational because of Daria's pregnancy?" I asked.

He sucked in a long breath and blew it out through pursed lips. "I had an affair with a parishioner. I admit" — he held up a hand, nearly choking on the words — "it was wrong. It was not going to solve the problem between Daria and me. And besides, I broke the vows I made to my wife before God." He smiled weakly. "But surely you can understand how powerful and confusing this kind of situation can be."

I was supposed to forgive him for cheating on his pregnant wife? I waited.

"I take full responsibility," he said into my chilly silence, pouting a little. "And it's cost me plenty. Daria insisted that I tell Reverend Wesley. He said that if I resigned without any fanfare, he would refrain from taking the issue public." His lips curled. "I hope she's happy with that now, because it was too late to get a profile together and apply for head pastor positions. Now I'm stuck with this for a year" — he spread his hands to take in the sloppy office — "which does not cover the bills generated by a wife and two children."

"That's why she took a job?"

He nodded. "Her mother helps with the twins three days a week. And those babies are a joy." He flashed a real smile and pushed a framed photograph of two infants across the desktop. They were dressed in fussy pink smocked dresses, with bald heads and toothless smiles.

"Beautiful," I said, handing the picture back. "Were you involved with Lacy?"

"My God no!" he yelped. "Oh my good God, you don't think I killed her?"

"I don't know what to think," I said, crossing my legs and leaning back in the chair.

He canted forward, his hands on his knees.

"Please understand, I can't tell you the name. Believe me, it wasn't Ms. Bailes."

"Was it Paul Cashman?"

His jaw dropped. "You've got to be kidding. Absolutely not! My God, where did you hear that?"

I shrugged. "I didn't hear it. I'm just trying to figure out what the hell is going on in our church."

"Listen," he said. "You have every right to judge me as a bad person. I abused the trust of both my wife and my lover. But I will not reveal her name. On that I'm quite clear. You can be sure that I've been thoroughly punished. And that I have pledged to refresh the vows I took during marriage with renewed vigor."

Fine. I was just glad I wasn't in Daria's shoes — two infants and a miserable straying bastard of a husband, wracked by his own guilt and disappointment and punishing her for it.

"Listen," I said. "Just for the record, you knew Reverend Wesley as well as anyone. Would you say he was capable of murder?"

Leo rubbed his chin. "Hard to picture that. He can get angry, but he's not a violent man."

Nodding shortly, I said my good-byes, apologizing for the impromptu visit and wishing him well. Underneath everything, Leo seemed to resent both Ellen and Paul as the candidates who might take over his treasured position. But he didn't appear to have done anything worse than offer a lukewarm recommendation for Ellen. And cheat on his wife. And betray the trust of his congregation.

CHAPTER 21

Outside, the leaden sky was releasing clumps of wet snow; already a half inch had settled on my car. My stomach growled. It was noon; not enough time to stop at the café on Main Street and get a real lunch, but no way I could make it to tea without food. I pulled up to a drive-thru McDonald's just off the interstate and ordered a cheeseburger, fries, and a Coke. The secret to enjoying a fast-food meal is squashing unsavory thoughts about what it might contain: E coli in the ground beef? Stop! French fries floating in trans fat? Why worry? Fourteen teaspoons of sugar? Just turn the radio volume up and gobble it down.

By the time I reached Northampton, visibility had worsened and a layer of slush was accumulating on the road. I squeezed the steering wheel, cursing at the vehicles that rushed by, spraying arcs of icy sludge onto my windshield. The wipers thwacked: *thud, thud, thud.* I turned off the radio and pushed myself to think about what I'd learned from Leo.

I'd pretty much scratched Leo himself off the list. And Wesley. It had always been difficult to picture Wesley as a killer, even though he'd found Lacy near death. But he did seem to have something going on with Paul. Something. Public figures have a way of thinking they're immune from the consequences of their own stupid actions. How do they convince themselves they'll never get caught? It shouldn't surprise me; the urges of the unconscious mind are unbelievably powerful, even when common sense and reason are furiously blinking caution. Like me breaking into Lacy's place. Twice. I grimaced.

Paul didn't strike me as much of a murder prospect either, though his behavior had been off-kilter ever since the church supper. Annabelle's cryptic E-mail about possible harassment added another layer. If Lacy had harassed him, might he have gone to her home to hash things out and what . . . thought to poison her cup of tea? Sounded stupid. As far as I knew, he didn't have a drinking problem like the person Lacy had apparently been speaking with right before she died. And ludicrous to picture Paul sabotaging himself by greasing the stairwell. The head injury was certainly not staged.

I started down another path. We'd had two attacks this week, carried out by two different methods. If we weren't counting the phantom gunshot at my condo, and apparently we weren't. The tea incident had to be carefully planned and was suitable for a killer with a weak stomach, as long as he got out before the poison kicked in. The other, the Crisco, seemed slapdash and unreliable: buckshot versus a sniper.

A car roared by inches away from me. I swerved and began to slide across the breakdown lane, gripping the steering wheel. The Honda lurched into a spin, and my mind with it. What would AAA remind me? No gas? More gas? Steer into the spin or away from it?

The car finally slid to a stop, halfway into the drainage ditch alongside the road. I kept my eyes squeezed shut for a few moments, heart beating wildly, waiting for a follow-up crash.

When nothing came, I pushed open the car door and climbed out of the Honda to survey the damage. My nerves were mangled, but the car seemed fine. I got back into the car, shifted it into gear, and tried to

289

pull back onto the highway. The tires only spun. I remembered loading two sacks of kitty litter into the trunk just days earlier. And I always carry a snow shovel. I dug at the snow around the tires, spread the litter, and gunned the motor. The tires gripped on the third try and I nosed back onto the highway. I tried to picture the car that caused me to spin out. Had it been only a careless driver in a rush to get home before the storm? Meigs was right — I was an idiot.

My hands were shaking, mouth dry, and stomach cramping. Could I cancel tea and go home to bed? I pictured the disappointment on Brittany's face and then the pinched look on my sister's. Forget it, not worth the trouble it would cause to reschedule. And right now, I needed to be with my family.

Two hours later, I pulled up in front of my sister's house on Randi Drive. I left the car running in the driveway and dashed up the walk. Brittany answered the door, dressed in a pink sweater and skirt edged in white fur and sprinkled with sequins. Her blond hair had been wrapped into a ballerina's topknot entwined with a strand of silver stars. She flung herself at me, arms open wide. Her white terrier leaped at my knees, barking furiously, the silver stars around his neck quivering.

"You look gorgeous — just like an angel!"

"Aunt Rebecca! Come and look at the tree!" She squirmed away and pulled me into the living room where Janice, with shoulders of steel, waited to grace me with an air kiss.

Brittany skipped around the tree, the dog tracking her footsteps. "O Christmas tree, O Christmas tree," she sang, pointing to her favorite ornaments like a little Vanna White. This year's theme was birds and their habitats — miniature birdhouses, silvery nests, delicate eggshells — it was stunning.

"It's beautiful," I said. "And mine is still naked. I'm going to need some help with that later. Let's hurry — we'll be late for our reservation." Janice bundled her into coat, hat, and mittens, and we dashed out to the car.

We parked on a side street in Madison and walked into the tea shop. The dining room was deserted.

"We have it all to ourself," Brittany whispered. A stern woman in a white apron handed us menus, recommending the afternoon tea. "Unless the child would prefer milk," she said, her mouth curling.

"Apricot tea and blueberry scones, double

on the clotted cream," I said, looking at Brittany for approval. She nodded and giggled. The server whisked away our menus.

Brittany squirmed in her seat and clasped her hands in front of her. "Ask me what I asked Santa for for Christmas," she said.

"What did you ask for from Santa?"

"It's a secret," she whispered.

"I won't tell," I whispered back.

"A sister!" she squealed, clapping her hands. "Won't Mommy be surprised?" She popped out of her chair, twirled like a ballerina, then spun back to her place.

"Wow. Yes, I bet she will." Would she ever. "Most of the time, the mommy and daddy have to decide something that big. Maybe you should ask for another Barb—"

"No, I don't want another Barbie," she said firmly. "I want a sister. You and Mommy have one. And when we say our prayers at night, she always says it's the most important thing in her life."

My eyes filled with quick tears just as the server approached our table with a heavy tray. She unloaded a pot of steaming apricot tea, a plate of scones, and bowls containing clotted cream and jam.

Brittany's eyes widened. "Whipped cream!"

I smiled and poured the tea, my heart grateful. We broke open our scones, Brittany chattering about her Sunday school holiday pageant. "All the boys get to be elves and the girls have to be angels. Do you think that's right?" She plopped four cubes of sugar into her teacup and stirred vigorously.

"I wonder if that might be a little too sweet?" I asked.

She fished one lump out with her spoon and deposited it on the saucer. The hot liquid sloshed over the edge of the china and seeped onto the tablecloth in a brown oval.

Our server swooped in, a hand towel ready. "My, my, you've really made a mess. Maybe they do it this way in France, but not in England." She whisked the saucer away, replaced it with a clean one from another table, and stalked back across the room.

Brittany flushed bright red and a tear started down her cheek. I patted her hand. "Don't worry, honey, that lady's just a grump." She nodded and snuffled, trying to smile through her tears. "Excuse me a minute? I'm going to nip into the ladies'. That's how we do it in England," I clowned in a fake British accent.

Shaking with fury, I marched across the room, pushed open the swinging door into the kitchen, and tapped the waitress's shoulder. "That young lady is your guest," I said in a low voice. "She has the best manners of any girl I know. But you won't get the opportunity to see that again because we will come back to this establishment when hell freezes over!"

I returned to the table, suddenly drenched with sweat and overwhelmed by a memory. I was four years old and I'd been waiting all day for my father to read to me. My mother had gone to bed early in the afternoon, instructing me to get my own supper and look after Janice. She had a classic and severe case of depression, I knew from my adult perspective. My father coming home from work was the light at the end of my tunnel.

"I'm sorry, Rebecca," he'd said when I showed him the book. "I have to take care of your mother. You understand that she's sick, don't you?"

He needed me to understand. I nodded.

Brittany and I sang Christmas carols in our new British accents on the way home — fueled by a dangerous combination of caffeine and sugar. Janice met us at the door and folded Brittany into a smothering hug.

"How was your tea?"

"Fine," she said, wiggling away to chase the dog. "We had two bowls of whipped cream."

"The server scolded her for spilling," I explained. "I hope it didn't ruin her time." I cleared my throat and smiled tentatively. "Can we kiss and make up? I hate fighting with you — especially at Christmas."

She glared. "Then maybe you can explain why you feel the need to turn this family upside down by dragging some miserable deserting-ass cheating bastard into the mix?"

I bristled back at her — then burst out laughing. I laughed until my stomach hurt and fell into Janice's open arms, both of us howling. I finally pulled away and wiped my eyes on the dish towel that hung over her shoulder.

"Don't even think about inviting him to Christmas dinner," she warned.

"You'll take this Bob guy at your table that I've met once and you won't have our father?" I patted her arm quickly. "Don't worry, he's in Thailand on sabbatical until spring. There's no danger of him showing up." I glanced at her grandfather clock. "Oh crap! I'm due at the church."

CHAPTER 22

In the church kitchen, Mrs. McCabe was stacking casserole dishes, empty and whistle clean, on a wheeled cart. The air was perfumed with their former contents, reminding me that it would be hell to face the committee working only on a greasy fast-food lunch and a blueberry scone, both gobbled under indigestion-boosting conditions.

"Good evening," I called. "Smells really great in here."

"Women's League Christmas supper," Mrs. McCabe said. "We served chicken divan, seven-layer salad, and brownies with peppermint ice cream. Everything except the brownies was red and green," she added proudly. "There's a little left over. Can I fix you a plate?"

I hesitated. She had a spot of sauce on her cheek and her thick brown hair frayed out from its careful twist. She looked tired. But I was ravenous. "If it's no trouble."

She opened the refrigerator, scooped a big serving of casserole onto a plate, and popped it into the microwave. Tipping her chin in the direction of the parlor, she asked: "Everything's going okay with your committee?"

"I suppose. I hope we'll make a decision tonight. It's been tough. Besides poor Lacy" — I was starting to use Leo's language — "the holidays always seem to stress folks out. People are so busy. They mean to enjoy the season, but it definitely adds more to your to-do list, doesn't it?"

She nodded. "I've been a member of this church for a long time — almost thirty-five years. Mr. McCabe and I were married here, you know." She bustled across the kitchen and ducked into her husband's office. I followed and she handed me a small, framed wedding photo. The newly minted Mr. and Mrs. had posed in front of the double stairs winding up to the pulpit. Mrs. McCabe wore a pillbox hat and carried a heart-shaped bouquet of white roses that looked like a box of expensive chocolates.

"You look beautiful," I said. "Love the flowers."

She took the photo back and went to replace it on the shelf in the office, behind two coiled extension cords, a black feather duster, and a glass jar full of screws and nuts.

"See this?" She patted the expanse of mirror glued to the wall behind the sexton's desk, now covered with photos, Post-its, and church announcements. "This room used to be the ladies' lounge," she said. "They touched up their lipstick in here."

"Wow," I said, "hard to imagine that." I backed out of the doorway so she could buzz back into the kitchen.

"This is one of the worst stretches our church has had," she said, blotting a wet spot on the stainless-steel countertop with her apron. "It's so difficult to see the good preachers come and go. Not to mention getting rid of the bad ones when you need to. Were you around before Reverend Wesley?"

"I'm a newcomer." I smiled. "Especially compared to you."

"I shouldn't say this, but the fellow before him was just awful," she said. "You can bet we all breathed a big sigh of relief when the good Lord called him somewhere else. But Reverend Wesley's a treasure. God willing, we'll keep him with us for a long, long time."

The microwave dinged and she pulled my steaming dinner out and added a helping of seven-layer iceberg lettuce salad, spackled with peas and red onion, heavy on the mayonnaise and cheese. She slid it onto the counter and handed me a fork and a paper napkin, wiping her hands on her apron. "You go on and take that into the parlor where you can relax," she said, grinning. "If Mr. McCabe complains about eating in his precious parlor, you send him to me."

I laughed. My mouth was watering. "Thanks so much."

"People don't realize how hard change is," she added. "They want change for the sake of change, and then later, they realize what they had and they're sorry."

I nodded and lifted the plate in salute. "Change is hard," I agreed.

I settled into the wing chair next to the couch and attacked the Women's League leftovers. Pieces of moist white meat nestled into a creamy sauce studded with broccoli and pimento. I could only find six layers in the salad — mayonnaise must be counted twice.

With my stomach full, the reality of the day was starting to seep in: the long drive, the scary spinout, losing my cool in the tea shop. Had the server really been rude enough to deserve the blasting I dished out? The incident reminded me of what I didn't have as a kid — someone to stick up for me. My eyes filled with tears and my tired brain reel replayed the footage of my father trudging up the stairs to take care of my mother, when I needed him too.

Detective Meigs and his sick wife shifted into focus: They were the perfect stand-ins for my old-time tableau. It wasn't that I wanted Meigs; I wanted a big bear of a father who would sometimes put me first, notwithstanding his sick wife. I could feel the tears and anger pressing but refused to knuckle under. Dammit, I would not melt down. I would finish up with the search committee as promised.

Babette and Mrs. Wiggett came in together, unwrapping parkas and scarves and wiping runny eyes and noses. "Another nasty night," said Mrs. Wiggett. "I hate to see what the rest of the winter's going to bring us."

"Poor little Wilson," said Babette. "The snowdrifts are twice his size already."

I pictured him hoisting his skinny little back leg, desperate for a target close to his height.

Barney burst into the room, red-faced, his hair and beard dusted with snow. "Sorry to be tardy," he blustered, though he didn't appear to be either.

Then Reverend Wesley rounded the corner

and reeled toward the couch, coughing hoarsely. I'd been hoping for a no-show.

"Shall we get started?" I asked. "I thought we might try something different. We'll each take a few minutes to talk about where we are in this process. Don't feel compelled to endorse one candidate or the other. Just give us your ideas about what's best for the church at this juncture, based on what we've heard so far. Would someone like to begin?"

"I'll start," said Mrs. Wiggett. "The only reasonable choice is Paul."

"Out of the question," said Barney. "You can't —"

"We're not arguing here," I interrupted. "The idea is that each of us gets the opportunity to speak freely, then we'll discuss once we've heard everyone out." He glowered. Mrs. Wiggett repeated her reasons for supporting Paul: youth, familiarity, performance as an intern. She'd clearly shifted away from both her concerns about his stress level and being railroaded by Wesley.

"Thank you," I said. "Now you, Barney?"

"Ellen Dark can provide what this church needs, not Paul. I will not vote for Paul Cashman. In fact, if the committee takes his nomination to the congregation, I will be forced to speak against him publicly."

Reverend Wesley broke in. "We must —"

I held my hand up. "You'll have your turn, sir. Babette?"

"I like Paul, I do," said Babette, wringing her hands. "On the other hand, Ellen doesn't bring any baggage —"

"So far as you know," barked Mrs. Wiggett, "which is not very far." The meeting deteriorated into noisy squabbling.

"Reverend Wesley?" I shouted waving my arms to penetrate the chaos. "What do you think?"

He paused until he had everyone's attention. "I'm going to call a congregational meeting," he said quietly, "and tell them the committee is deadlocked. I'm going to tell the people that it's in their hands directly and that I recommend hiring Paul. Thank you all for your time and effort, but I believe we have to move on." He raised his eyes to the portrait on the wall, nodded good night, and walked out.

"He can't do that," sputtered Mrs. Wiggett. "Can he?"

"We have to get our hands on a copy of the bylaws," Barney said. "Or call the central office." He plucked at the pocket watch hanging from his belt loop. "No one will be there tonight. This is simply unacceptable. He can't do an end run around us

— we are the church's elected representatives."

The two began to plot their counterattack. Finally something had drawn them together. I sank back, my chin on my chest, stunned and drained. Was this the plan all along? Had Wesley set me up the whole way? Had me meant me to believe I had the ability to help formulate the committee's decision, when he knew they were incapable of agreeing on anything?

"We'll be in touch tomorrow," said Barney, rising. I wiggled my fingers to signal good night.

"Shall I wait and walk you out?" Babette asked timidly, watery blue eyes blinking faster and faster.

"I'm just going to sit here a moment," I said. "Thanks."

I stayed in the wing chair until everyone left, snapping the rubber band on my wrist and telling myself to let it go. But the rage swelled until I couldn't contain it.

I grabbed my coat, slammed the parlor door shut tight, and hurried outside. Picking through the footsteps in the snow across the green, I followed Wesley's path to the parsonage. His gait was longer than mine and I didn't want to risk turning my weak ankle again. Just ahead, the lights in his kitchen twinkled on.

A desiccated pine wreath with a crumpled red bow — the youth mission trip fundraiser — had been hung on the oak door. I stamped my feet on the mat, rang the bell, and banged on the door. A cloud of needles fell off the wreath and dropped to the stoop in a gust of forest-scented air. Shuffling footsteps echoed in the front hallway. The door cracked open. One of Wesley's eyes peered out from the dark space behind.

"Rebecca Butterman?" he said in surprise, opening the door a little wider. "Is something wrong?"

"You're damn right," I said, pushing forward across the threshold, ready to force my way in and pin him to the mat. "Can I come in? We need to talk."

I was sure I heard him groan. But he swung open the door and led the way to the living room. This was the first time I'd seen the inside of the parsonage since Beverly left. It looked sad and bare: faded oblongs of paint on the walls where pictures had hung and the shelves emptied of knick-knacks. A cheap faux-wood rolling table held a wide-screen TV, picture on, volume low.

"What can I do for you?" he asked.

"Frankly, I've had it," I said. "You dragged

me out of bed in the middle of the night to run a pastoral search committee. You insisted that I was the only one who could handle the job. So I did it as a favor to you and to the church. From the beginning, you have not allowed us to do our work. Jesus himself could be in charge and you wouldn't trust the process."

"If I took Barney aside and asked him to resign —"

"No!" My voice shrilled into shrieking harridan range.

Wesley shrunk back into the couch.

"You haven't come clean with me since Lacy's murder. Either you tell me now exactly what's going on, or I go to the council," I warned. "I'm sorry to be harsh, but we can't make a fair choice this way. I'm going to strongly recommend that we ditch what we've done so far and start over. With a new committee. Of reasonable people."

Wesley's face paled, highlighting the dark shadows of his late-night whiskers. "No," he said. "You can't do that."

"Then you tell me why." Stifling a sudden twinge of fear, I sat back and crossed one leg over the other.

He dropped his head into his hands. "Because I'm going to resign on January first, and we have to have someone in place to run the show." He straightened slowly. "Paul knows the church and the people. He'll be able to manage until we hire a head pastor. We can't have a total stranger — it will already be chaos."

For a moment I just gaped at him. "You're resigning?" I finally managed. "Why?"

"Beverly." He spread his hands wide, delicate fingers looking helpless in the flashing light of the TV screen. "She has a gambling problem. I tried to help her, but she ran up an unfathomable debt on our credit card." His brave smile crumpled. "I didn't know how to get out of the mess we were in." His shoulders heaved silently with his breathing.

This was no time to retreat. "And so?"

"I borrowed from the minister's discretionary fund. It was only nine thousand to clear the decks so that Beverly could leave. I tried to help her," he said again. "We went to a Gamblers Anonymous meeting in Bridgeport but she said she wouldn't go back. I offered to attend couples' therapy but that went nowhere too. So I had to give her an ultimatum: You either get help or you have to go. She chose to go." His face was still as chiseled marble and his voice, just that cold. "I have every intention of paying the money back — in fact, I've already started."

"Who else knows?" I asked.

"Paul knows."

"Paul?" I asked. "Did Paul blackmail you in exchange for your support?"

He rose quickly. "Absolutely not! I was attending the quarterly meeting at central office and Mrs." — he blinked — "never mind who — one of our people called in a panic. They were going to shut off her electric that day, whether she had babies in her house or not. Nancy passed the message onto Paul. He didn't want to promise we could help if there wasn't any money in the fund. So he went into my desk for the checkbook and he noticed the missing check and the amount in the register." Wesley wrung his hands. "Poor kid, he was so embarrassed to bring it up. I explained that it had been a desperate mistake, a very human error. Then I showed him the deposits I was already making and told him I had decided to resign."

"Anybody else know?" I asked, trying to process all this, thinking suddenly of Lacy.

"I certainly haven't told anyone. And Paul's been sworn to secrecy. He didn't mention it to Nancy." He scowled. "Who knows what Beverly told Leo."

"Told . . . Leo?"

"After we talked, I assumed you'd figured it out." His face reddened.

"Oh, you're joking." I puffed out a big breath of air. "Leo had his affair with Beverly?"

He nodded.

I'd given Leo a little credit for protecting the identity of his lover — now it simply looked like a case of covering his ass.

"Did you ask Leo to leave?"

Wesley nodded again. "We couldn't continue to work together. I told him I would keep quiet if he resigned quickly."

"Did you have an affair with Lacy?"

He jerked back and yelped. "Of course not! Why would you even say that?"

"The whooping cough symptoms," I said.

"I swear," he laid his hand on his chest, "we didn't get any closer than a handshake."

"Then what does all this have to do with Lacy's murder?" I asked.

"I don't know," he moaned, looking suddenly boneless and exhausted. "I went to her house on Friday to beg her to support Paul. But she was so sick. And you know the rest. Oh God, I feel awful about all this. Look, do you mind if we continue this conversation tomorrow? I do want your input on how to handle the situation, but right now I can't even think."

I squeezed his hand — he pulled away when I made a move to hug him. More pine needles fell from the wreath as I left the parsonage; it would be a ring of bare branches by Christmas. I retraced my steps across the green, feeling wrung out. The moon had risen, casting ghostly light and shadows on the snow. The image of my bed materialized like a homing device. And Spencer. Warm, furry, purring Spencer.

I couldn't begin to imagine the depth of Wesley's humiliation. A man in that position, cuckolded by his assistant, reduced to stealing — call it borrowing, if you want — from the church fund used to help the neediest people. My breath caught. What if Wesley really had killed Lacy? I glanced behind me, but the expanse of green was empty. Wesley had the biggest motivation of all: hiding his mortifying fall from head pastor at a historic church to — well, just another embarrassed, misguided, and washed-up clergyman. I couldn't wait to get home and unload the whole mess onto Meigs.

In the fellowship hall parking lot, I patted my pockets for my keys. But in the hurry to confront Wesley, I'd left my purse in the parlor. Now I could picture exactly where it was, stashed between the fainting couch and the wing chair. No purse? No keys. No cell phone. No way home.

But like all the other committee chairs, I'd been given the combination to the lock-box of the Fellowship Hall. I tapped the numbers in sequence and the door clicked open. The red exit sign glowed just brightly enough to allow me to flip the toggle on the wall. Fluorescent bulbs flickered on down the length of the hallway and I breathed a sigh of relief. I tiptoed past the kitchen to the parlor and flipped that light on too. Yes, there was my handbag. I picked it up off the floor, dug out the keys, and slid them into my coat pocket.

Exiting the parlor, I heard footsteps tapping up the stairs from the basement. I ducked into the kitchen, suddenly very afraid. The footsteps came closer, I faded into the shadows of the cupboards near the sexton's office.

A man came around the corner, nearly slamming into me.

I screamed, then clapped my hand to my chest. "Oh my God, Paul, you scared me half to death!"

CHAPTER 23

"What are you doing here?" I gasped.

"I always check the stove on my way out." He grinned and touched my shoulder. "Sorry for the scare. Some of those League ladies aren't so young anymore. I worry they'll leave the gas burner on and blow us all to heaven's gate — before we're ready to go. But what are *you* doing here?" His shoulders slumped and one hand strayed to his forehead where the bandage had been. "How did the meeting go tonight?"

"Not very well. And I've just come from the parsonage," I said, eyes narrowing. "Wesley told me about how you found the checkbook. And how you promised to lie for him."

Paul flushed a bright red. "I didn't lie. I swore I wouldn't say anything, to give him time to do the right thing." He ran his hand over his face. "You can feel so isolated as a minister. Who can you really talk to if you're down or angry or in despair?"

I bit back my first thought: *You're of no use at all if you can't ask for help when you need it.*

"This isn't the kind of issue you should have tried to handle on your own," I scolded. "It makes me worry for you, Paul. When you're responsible for a congregation's welfare, you have to know when to go for help."

"I did go for help," he said firmly. Then his voice cracked. "I went to Lacy."

"Sit down," I said, steering him into the sexton's office. He plopped into the desk chair. I stood over him, arms across my chest. "Tell me what happened. You saw her the night of the murder?"

He nodded, near tears. "She was *fine* when I saw her. She was *alive*."

"What time was this? Did she seem upset? Did you notice anything off in her house, or in her manner?" I knew I was pelting the poor kid with questions, but I couldn't believe he'd kept all this to himself. "Did you talk to the cops?"

"I couldn't," he pleaded. "I'd promised. And I swear, I didn't see anything. She took a ton of notes like the first time we talked, and then I left. I swear I was there for fifteen

312

minutes, no more. I was back in my car by six."

"You discussed this with her more than once?"

He nodded.

"Why Lacy?"

His words fell out in an anxious rush. "I knew her a little because we'd chatted about the search and whether I should apply for the job. She had a lot of business experience and she struck me as no-nonsense. I thought I could trust her."

"But?"

"She was horrified about what Reverend Wesley had done," he admitted, wincing. He tugged his earlobes. "She was totally against the idea of handling this privately. She said secrets are poison — she'd learned that in AA. She said she'd have to take it to the church council herself if Wesley or I didn't. She agreed to wait until the first of January to see if I managed to persuade Wesley to come clean."

"So Wesley went there Friday night to discuss his resignation?" I asked.

He shrugged, looking green and queasy. "Either that or hiring me. But she didn't believe I could lead the congregation properly starting out on a lie." He moved his fingers to the pulse point on his neck.

"Sadly, I've come to the conclusion she was right."

"If she was killed because someone didn't want Wesley to be found out, wouldn't you be in danger too?"

We stared at each other, realizing what I'd just said. I whistled softly, looking around the office and trying to fit the pieces together. Who cared that much about Wesley's reputation? Wesley himself, of course. Beverly? She hadn't been sighted in weeks, maybe months. From the sounds of it, she was mired in the depths of her own addiction and hardly concerned about him.

"Paul," I said. "I'm afraid it was Wesley."

My gaze fell on a Hummel figurine, just visible behind the wedding photo on Mr. McCabe's shelf. I heard a soft clang in the kitchen, like a coat zipper hitting metal, and swung around to find Mrs. McCabe standing in the doorway, training a gun on Paul.

"Move over next to the young man," she said. "Or I blow him to pieces." She smiled humorlessly.

Paul began to hyperventilate and then to sniffle. I shuffled closer to him, hardly believing what was happening.

"Mrs. McCabe," I got out. "It's only me and Paul."

"For the love of God," Mrs. McCabe

snapped at the sniveling Paul, "take a deep breath and act like a man."

"Mrs. McCabe," I said more firmly, "you don't want to hurt us, I know you don't. Suppose we set the gun aside and just talk. Just between us."

"I'm sorry to have to take it this far," she said. "But the only two people who know about the checkbook are right here. And it simply can't go any further. If Reverend Wesley can't defend himself, then I'll do it for him."

Okay, I told myself. She's not thinking like a killer, she's thinking like a frantic lover or mother — anything to protect her chick. Which in this case must be Reverend Wesley. A bizarre image, but I wasn't going to argue.

"Wesley will resign anyway," I announced with more conviction than I felt. "Even if we disappear."

"He'll have to stay on." The wattles under her chin wobbled with the force of her nod. "He won't have a choice — it's what's best for the church."

I snuck a glance sideways at Paul, whose mouth hung half open. "But why?" he finally asked. "Mrs. McCabe, let's be reasonable. Why is this worth killing two more people?"

She jutted her chin out, a scary light in her eyes. "Reverend Wesley brought this church back to life. This church is nothing if he leaves, nothing. I won't allow that awful woman's sins to drive him off."

Beverly, I guessed she meant.

"Did you spread the Crisco?" I asked. If we delayed her long enough, a good idea might come, either to me or to Paul. Or *some* idea.

"Don't you write an advice column?" asked Mrs. McCabe. "What would Dr. Smarty-Pants say about minding your own damn business?"

I pushed on. "Why hurt Paul?"

The gun wavered and she supported the left hand with the right and glared at him. "I heard you talking in Reverend Wesley's office." She swung the gun and her gaze back to me. "At first I thought everything would work out okay. That horrid bitch dug a hole for him, but Paul would help him climb back out." She narrowed her eyes to angry slits. "Then Mr. Honest-and-Aboveboard got the big idea of talking to Lacy Bailes. She wrote it all down — every word. I found the notes when I cleaned house," she spat at Paul. "You were cracking up: You couldn't be relied on to protect Wesley. You didn't have the backbone to carry it off. I could see that."

"I know Wesley," Paul stammered. "He'll never be able to serve the church under these conditions. He's made up his mind about leaving. He'd decided that before I even talked with him about the irregularity with the money."

"He borrowed money from the discretionary fund," I said gently. "He knows that was a terrible error in judgment. We all respect him for doing the right thing."

Mrs. McCabe drew her eyebrows together and scowled. "We're going out to the Dumpster," she said. The gun in her hands was trembling but her expression was pure determination. A crazy light infused her eyes and glowed in her face. She looked like a besotted lover.

"So you went out to Lacy's home Friday night to make your case for Reverend Wesley — and Paul," I said. "Instead, she began to talk with you about your own drinking problem. While she was on the phone with Roger, you made the tea and put the lily of the valley in hers."

"Don't think I won't shoot you," she said. "The sexton taught me to use this gun and I will do it — without missing this time."

"It was you the other night!"

Mrs. McCabe wouldn't look at me. "Take

the yellow extension cord off the hook on the shelf and tie him up," she said.

I reached for the cord. "You should think of your husband, what this will do to him," I tried.

"He's in his own little world," she said. "He'll never even notice. He thinks he runs the church." Droplets of spittle sprayed out and hit Paul in the face.

"This is never going to work," I pleaded. "One of the neighbors is sure to hear you."

"We're going down to the basement," she said. "Can't hear a thing down there, right, Paul?"

"What will you possibly do with . . . the bodies?" *Our* bodies.

Mrs. McCabe moved the gun to her left hand and pointed to the pack of plastic garbage bags on the bottom shelf. "Super strength," she said. "Mr. McCabe won't buy anything that'll bust halfway out to the Dumpster and spill garbage across the parking lot. There's a wheelbarrow in the basement. Trash man comes tomorrow. And don't think I haven't lifted plenty of heavy sacks into that bin. Neither one of you weighs much to speak of." She clicked off the safety. "Move it. We don't have all night."

"Turn around," I said to Paul. He stepped

to the left, his arms held behind him. I began to wind the cord around his wrists in a lazy figure eight.

"Tighter!" she said. "And hurry!"

As I worked — the cord was too long and too thick for the job, and damn slippery — my eyes searched the small space wildly for any sort of weapon. Despite the kitchen's energy-saving chill, my hairline and armpits were damp with effort and fear.

"That'll do," said Mrs. McCabe. Paul jerked his head up, pupils wide with terror. "Let's get going."

He started to the door, with me one step behind. I grabbed the spade I'd seen angled in the corner, swung around, and swatted hard at her arm. She screamed and the gun skittered across the floor and slid under the stove. I shoved Paul out into the center of the kitchen, sending him sprawling onto the waxed floor. I slammed the office door and locked Mrs. McCabe inside.

"Get up and run!" I squawked, tugging on his arm.

CHAPTER 24

I gripped the extension cord and hauled Paul to his feet. Together we stumbled out of the church hall and trotted to the car. I spent a few desperate moments trying to untie the cord. It wasn't coming loose so Paul fell into my Honda, hands still tied behind his back. We peeled out of the parking lot, stopping just long enough to speak to Officer Scott, posted at the bottom of the hill.

"Lacy Bailes's murderer is locked in the sexton's office!" I shrieked, and drove off at top speed to the police department. No way I was waiting at the church for Mrs. McCabe to do a Houdini and reappear with her pistol. My heart was still thumping at the idea of the black bag in the Dumpster. Didn't she think someone would find the bodies? It wouldn't have mattered — we'd have already been dead.

We burst into the police station lobby, me

gripping Paul's bound arm. "Mrs. Mary McCabe is locked in her husband's office at the Shoreline Congregational Church," I said to the dispatcher. "She's the one who killed Lacy Bailes."

"She tried to kill us too!" Paul yelped.

The dispatcher confirmed that backup squad cars were on the way to the church and then phoned Detective Meigs.

"Dr. Butterman is here again," she said. "And she's with a Paul Cashman who is tied up with some kind of cord." Her voice dropped low. "They claim to have solved the Bailes murder."

Officer Kent came out to the lobby to collect us, the expression on his face flat.

"Were you in the Scouts?" he asked me as he worked Paul's hands free. He almost smiled. "These knots are impressive."

Then he settled us in a conference room with cardboard cups of bad coffee. Fifteen minutes later, Detective Meigs entered the room. I scrambled to my feet.

"We've got her in custody. Looks like you broke her arm," he said, sighing heavily.

"She had it coming," Paul muttered, rubbing his wrist and then touching his head where the bandage had been. Meigs smiled faintly.

"Start at the top," said Meigs, his smile

fading. He perched one butt cheek on the corner of the conference table, leg swinging.

So I told him about the search committee's collapse and how I'd stormed over to confront Reverend Wesley. "Listen, I had no intention of going back into the building, but my keys were inside. I had no way to get home."

Meigs looked unconvinced.

I suppressed the urge to snap his head off. Maybe I had made other boneheaded choices over the last week, but that decision was easy.

"My purse was right where I'd left it. But then I heard footsteps in the stairwell. I've been feeling so jumpy lately, I just — I ducked into the kitchen. Luckily it was only Paul. We were talking about the case" — I wished I could take the words back as soon as I said them — "when Mrs. McCabe came around the corner holding a gun."

"She fully intended to shoot us and put us out with the trash!" Paul broke in. "She told us that herself!"

"Let's hear the rest," said Meigs, rolling his head toward one shoulder, then the other.

"Mrs. McCabe adored Reverend Wesley. Not in a sexualized kind of way," I added quickly. "Well, who knows what was really on her mind. Unconsciously, I mean."

Meigs gestured impatiently for me to get on with it.

"She hated the idea of adapting to a new minister. And she reached the point where she'd do anything to protect him so he could remain at the church. But his wife Beverly buried him in debt."

I let Paul tell the story about Reverend Wesley's financial problems and how he'd borrowed from the ministerial discretionary fund.

"I couldn't believe it when I saw the notation in the checkbook register," said Paul. "Beverly." He shook his head. "I tried to explain it away to myself. When I couldn't think of another solution, I talked with my adviser at the divinity school. She suggested hashing the problem over with Lacy Bailes."

His eyes filled and I patted his hand. He obviously felt responsible for her death, and what could I say about that? In the end, Beverly and Wesley had set the ugly chain of events in motion. But Paul would have to come to terms with his participation.

"Mrs. McCabe went to Lacy's home on Friday night to make one last pitch to protect her Wesley. When she saw the notes on Lacy's consultation with Paul," I said, "she decided she had to destroy Lacy, along with all her evidence."

"Did you visit Miss Bailes right after dark on the night she died?" Meigs asked sternly.

Paul lowered his head. "I'm sorry I didn't come forward. I didn't know what to do. Lacy promised to hold off saying anything until after New Year's. That would give the reverend enough time to do the right thing, she said."

"You didn't think we needed to have this piece of information?" Meigs voice was deathly quiet.

"I wanted to give Wesley time to do what he needed to do," Paul said stubbornly.

"Including set you up as the next minister?" Meigs asked. Paul blanched.

"He feels bad enough already without you haranguing him," I said to Meigs.

The detective frowned. "Then Mrs. McCabe tried to kill you with Crisco?"

"I suspect she was pickled that night," I interrupted. "And way past the point of logical thinking. I did smell alcohol on someone's breath — I thought it was Mrs. Wiggett." I snickered and turned to Paul. "I should have guessed when she referred to you as a hunka hunka burnin' love."

Paul turned bright red. "In the end, she didn't trust me not to leak all this to the authorities."

Meigs grunted. "None of this says much for the guy you were trying to protect."

"There's no bad guy here," Paul said, and then quickly added, "except for Mrs. Mc-Cabe. And she thought she was doing the right thing too."

"This is why we have laws and cops," said Meigs. "So every moron isn't out there making his own rules."

Paul looked away. "He was just a regular good person who took one wrong turn."

"Wouldn't you think a minister should be held to a higher standard than the rest of us?" Meigs asked. "Don't you guys take some kind of vow?"

Paul grimaced, lips pressed thin in his pale face. "Maybe we should be expected to be more attentive. But in the end, a minister's only a person. Like a shrink, right?" He tried a smile in my direction.

I nodded. "You can be in a situation and absolutely recognize that there's an under-tow of feelings and history, and still get pulled under." I raised my eyes and met Meigs's brown ones. Paul looked down at his hands.

"Maybe . . ." I swallowed. "Maybe the trick is knowing when not to go into the water at all."

CHAPTER 25

Friday night, Christmas Eve, Brittany and Janice stopped in to help me decorate the crooked tree. The branches twinkled with tinsel, a few ornaments, and tiny white lights — I'd put the new jumbo-sized bulbs on the bushes outside, in Mrs. Dunbarton's honor. To celebrate a job well done, we were nibbling on melt-away cookies — recipe courtesy of Esther Tuborg.

Janice leaned back and sighed, a snifter of Courvoisier in one hand and a chocolate-dipped, confectioner's sugar–coated cookie in the other. "There's one thing left." She directed Brittany to drag the dog-eared cardboard box out from under the tree where I'd stashed it after our fight.

"You open it for me," I told Brittany.

"Carefully," instructed Janice.

Brittany unfolded the cardboard flaps and began to unwind yellowed tissue paper from the objects inside. They were old family ornaments: handblown glass elves and Santas, crocheted stars, baby pictures rimmed with doilies and glued to sterling silver shapes, tarnished with age. Brittany began to hang them on my tree.

"I don't have to take all of them," I said, hiding a smile, knowing they'd never find a place on Janice's carefully orchestrated masterpiece.

"I found the box in the attic," Janice said, tapping the cardboard on the coffee table with one long red fingernail. "You can hand them off to Brittany when you're ready."

"I love them," I said, reaching over to hug her. "Thank you. Anytime *you're* ready, I'm happy to share."

Brittany held up a loose photo of our smiling parents, baby Janice tucked in the crook of our mother's arm.

"Who are these people? Am I this baby?" she asked.

I answered the easier question. "That baby is your mom."

"That's your mommy and daddy?" she asked Janice.

Janice put her hand to her throat, her eyes moist, and nodded.

"When can we see them?" Brittany asked. "You said you'd tell me about them when I was older."

Suddenly bright red and speechless, Janice fanned her face and motioned to me for help.

"Our mother died a long time ago," I said, mustering a warm smile for my niece. "She's up in Heaven. She watches out for us every day."

"She's dead?" Brittany cried, throwing herself into her own mother's lap.

"It's okay. She died a long time ago," said Janice. She stroked her daughter's hair. "But we still miss her."

Brittany bounced up and sprung onto the couch. "Then I'll meet your daddy?"

"We'll see," said Janice. She glanced at her watch. "Oh my gosh, look at the time. Your daddy will be waiting. We're going to the Shepards' for supper, then Brittany's an angel in the pageant. See you there?"

"Yes, see you later," I said, not willing to explain why I might need a break from church, even if it wasn't my own.

I helped them into their coats, hugged and kissed them out into the cold night, and collapsed on the sofa. The doorbell rang as soon as I had my feet up and Spencer settled on my stomach. I groaned and rolled him off to the side.

"What did you forget this time?" I said as I threw open the door. But it wasn't my sister, it was my ex, holding a small silver box. I froze.

"Can I come in for a minute?" Mark finally asked. He wore a blue wool blazer and a gingham-checked shirt under the camel-hair overcoat. Had he dressed up for me? More likely, a date.

"Sorry." I shuffled aside. "I'm surprised to see you, that's all."

"I wanted to wish you a happy holiday," he said. "I should say Merry Christmas." He smiled sheepishly and held out the package.

"Same to you. I just finished decorating the tree. With Janice and Brittany," I added inanely.

"How are they?" Mark glanced behind me at the tree, looking sad. "So . . . you're really — moving on."

I couldn't think of anything to say. "I'm working on it," I said. "Isn't that why we got divorced?"

"I guess so," he said. "Aren't you going to open the package?"

I fumbled with the wrapping — a professional job — and lifted off the lid. A deep red stone winked in the center of a nest, woven of delicate strands of silver. I stared at the pin and back up at him.

"It's a garnet," he said. "Your birthstone."

"Thank you," I said. "I'm speechless. It's stunning."

"I should have given it to you when we were married," he said, and kissed me on the cheek.

I nodded dumbly, still staring at the box.

"Merry Christmas," he said softly, and left.

I watched Mark drive off in his BMW, then pulled on my coat and boots and slogged down the street and around the corner to the town dock. The wind moaned, whipping up snow eddies from the drifts, the cold cutting through to the bone. It was snowing again, sharp needles that pricked my cheeks and made my eyes water. No one in her right mind would be out here tonight.

I paused at the boat ramp, stamping my feet. Why had Mark shown up with that gorgeous pin? All the years we were married, he'd given me anonymous household items like a steam iron and a George Foreman. I reminded myself that it didn't matter what the meaning was for *him,* as long as I had truly moved on.

The night was black; just enough light reflected from the street lamp that I could make out the dark shape of the abandoned house across the inlet. It was a faded red — I'd seen it a thousand times in the daylight.

Whoever had lived there once was long gone by now, the loves in her life probably dead too. My teeth began to chatter and I turned and hurried toward home.

I scooped a medium-sized bowl of chocolate ice cream, poured another splash of cognac, and curled up on the couch. Spencer hopped up and butted the computer with his head.

"Cats don't eat chocolate," I said, moving the bowl to the other side of the coffee table. Then I started to type Dr. Aster's end-of-the-year advice column.

Dear Dr. Aster:
With January fast approaching, I'm thinking about New Year's resolutions. And I realized that I haven't kept a single one from last year! I'm still fat, in a dead-end job, and attracted to losers. Any suggestions for more success this year?
Sincerely,
Discouraged in Detroit

Dear Discouraged:
Dr. Aster feels your pain! In fact, gyms count on an influx of eager customers in January and then a precipitous drop-off in attendance,

knowing how fast good intentions fade. After all, February is cold and dark and you've worked a long day — wouldn't it feel a whole lot better to serve yourself a bowl of chocolate ice cream and slip into bed?

Big goals are important, but they can be impossible to achieve unless you break them down into smaller steps. Reach out to your inner gym rat by starting with a class that sounds like fun and meets just one night a week. Sign up with a buddy so when you're feeling unmotivated, she can drag you along. And try a single small change in your current eating habits — maybe designate one night as a "no dessert" zone. This way you're cutting down on calories little by little and upping your metabolism without feeling deprived.

Now the man problem, hmmm. This may require a little more introspection. Can you spot a pattern in the way you've gotten stuck? Falling for married men would be one obvious example, or sticking with guys who make it clear they have no intention of settling down. Assuming that's what you want . . .

The doorbell rang. I set the laptop and the empty ice cream bowl on the coffee table and crossed the room to peer through the peephole in my front door. It was Meigs; his reddish curls were slicked back behind his ears and he too was carrying a package. I was surprised to see him, if *surprised* applies to a mixture of astonishment . . . and unwelcome pleasure.

"You're busy," he said when he saw the laptop on the coffee table. "Sorry to interrupt."

"Come on in," I said. "Let me take your coat. Can I get you a drink? Or a cookie?"

"Can't stay," he said, setting the package on my coffee table. "Just wanted to follow up on Mrs. McCabe. She'll be in detox for ten days, then off to jail. Her lawyer's arguing to get her murder rap reduced to manslaughter. Doubt that'll fly. She's insisting she was drunk when she got to Lacy's house. Then when the conversation went sour, she panicked and cooked up the poison tea."

I shook my head. "Poor Lacy. She was a good woman who tried so hard. You'd think Mr. McCabe would have paid more attention to how desperate his wife was feeling."

"Denial's a powerful thing." Meigs's neck reddened and the color spread right on up

333

through his ears. "So I'm told. I also wanted you to know that I took your advice."

"My advice?" I asked, dumfounded.

He laughed, pointing to the computer. "Isn't that your specialty?"

"Oh, Dr. Aster, yes. But I wouldn't expect you to listen to me about anything." I cleared my throat. "What advice did I give you?"

He looked embarrassed all over again. "Don't you remember? In the cemetery? You suggested we should go for marriage counseling."

"Of course." I nodded, struggling to keep my expression blank. Of course I wanted him to work things out with his sick wife. What kind of disturbed wack job wouldn't want that?

"She's still sick — it doesn't change that," he continued, pleating his lower lip between his fingers. "Nothing can change that. But we're closer than we've ever been. We have you to thank."

"You're welcome," I said.

"The counselor feels a lot of the trouble between us has to do with my being a cop."

"And how do you feel about that?" I asked automatically. Then I tapped my cheek and smiled. "Sorry. None of my damn business."

"I think she's right. By the time I get

home from chasing bad guys" — he made air quotes with his fingers — "from taking care of everything outside, there isn't a whole lot left." He rubbed his chin. "It's not that Alice was asking too much. It's that she was asking anything. She only wanted what she thought I'd promised: a big lug to take care of her."

I willed away a rush of awkwardness: I wanted the same damn thing.

He zipped his jacket closed and pointed to the clumsily wrapped gift. "That's for you."

"I didn't expect . . . I didn't get you anything." Truly, it hadn't crossed my mind.

He shrugged. "I saw this at a tag sale last week and thought of you. It's nothing."

I untied the ribbon and tore open the paper, white with red candy canes all over. And a lot of Scotch tape. He'd found a signed first edition of Fannie Flagg's original *Farmhouse Cookbook.* I'd seen it on an eBay auction earlier in the month. It went for six hundred and change. No way he picked this up at the bargain table at a tag sale. A tag sale during the coldest December on record? I didn't think so.

"I'm speechless," I said for the second time in one night. "Thank you."

"Merry Christmas," he said. He leaned

over, touched his lips to my forehead, and walked out.

Shutting the door behind him, I pulled the drapes away from the window and watched him stride down the front walk. He hopped into his minivan — left running — and sped away, tires squealing. Things could be worse, I told myself, and summoned up an image of Mrs. McCabe sitting in a cell. She'd wanted something she couldn't have too. And she hadn't even known it. I shivered.

New Year's resolution number four hundred and two: Learn to want what's in front of you. Available.

I went into the kitchen, Spencer at my heels, and dialed Bob's number. He answered on the first ring.

"It's Rebecca Butterman. This isn't the most glamorous invitation, but I wondered if you'd like to go to the Madison Congregational Church's Christmas pageant? It's in half an hour. My niece is an angel . . ."

"I'd love to," he said without hesitating. "Maybe we can grab a bite to eat after that."

I hung up the phone, grinning, and brought Spencer's empty water dish to the sink. I glanced out the window and noticed two cars pulling up in front of Mrs. Dunbarton's condo — a no-parking zone. She'd be out to correct that in minutes.

Teenagers wearing Santa hats but no coats tumbled out of the cars, laughing and talking. They jostled up her walkway and rang the doorbell, the lead teen turning to shush the others. I smiled widely as Mrs. Dunbarton swung her door open to receive my Secret Santa gift. I could just picture her scolding face transformed by surprise.

"God rest ye, Mrs. Dunbarton, may nothing you dismay . . ." the teenagers sang.

ABOUT THE AUTHOR

Anthony and Agatha Award nominee **Roberta Isleib** is a clinical psychologist who lives with her family in Connecticut. Visit her Web site at www.robertaisleib.com or E-mail her at Roberta@robertaisleib.com.

We hope you have enjoyed this Large Print book. Other Thorndike, Wheeler, and Chivers Press Large Print books are available at your library or directly from the publishers.

For information about current and upcoming titles, please call or write, without obligation, to:

Publisher
Thorndike Press
295 Kennedy Memorial Drive
Waterville, ME 04901
Tel. (800) 223-1244

or visit our Web site at:

http://gale.cengage.com/thorndike

OR

Chivers Large Print
published by BBC Audiobooks Ltd
St James House, The Square
Lower Bristol Road
Bath BA2 3SB
England
Tel. +44(0) 800 136919
email: bbcaudiobooks@bbc.co.uk
www.bbcaudiobooks.co.uk

All our Large Print titles are designed for easy reading, and all our books are made to last.